Rosa Nouchette Carey

Uncle Max

Vol. I

Rosa Nouchette Carey

Uncle Max
Vol. I

ISBN/EAN: 9783743373846

Manufactured in Europe, USA, Canada, Australia, Japa

Cover: Foto ©Andreas Hilbeck / pixelio.de

Manufactured and distributed by brebook publishing software (www.brebook.com)

Rosa Nouchette Carey

Uncle Max

BY

ROSA NOUCHETTE CAREY

AUTHOR OF 'NELLIE'S MEMORIES' 'NOT LIKE OTHER GIRLS' 'WEE WIFIE'

IN THREE VOLUMES

VOL. I.

LONDON

RICHARD BENTLEY & SON, NEW BURLINGTON STREET

Publishers in Ordinary to Her Majesty the Queen

1887

CONTENTS

OF

THE FIRST VOLUME.

UNCLE MAX.

CHAPTER I.

OUT OF THE MIST.

T appears to me, looking back over a past experience, that certain days in one's life stand out prominently as landmarks, when we arrive at some finger-post pointing out the road that we should follow.

We come out of some deep, rutty lane, where the hedgerows obscure the prospect, and where the footsteps of some unknown passenger have left tracks in the moist red clay. The confused tracery of green leaves overhead seems to weave fanciful patterns against the dim blue of the sky; the very air is low-pitched and oppressive. All at once we find ourselves in an open space; the free winds of heaven are blowing over us ; there are four roads meeting ; the finger-post points silently, ' This way to such a place ;' we can take our choice, counting the milestones rather wearily as we pass them. The road may be a little tedious, the stones may hurt our feet; but if it be the right road it will bring us to our destination.

In looking back it always seems to me as though I came to a fresh landmark in my experience that November afternoon when I saw Uncle Max standing in the twilight, waiting for me.

There had been the waste of a great trouble in my young life—sorrow, confusion, then utter chaos. I had struggled on somehow after my twin brother's death, trying to fight against despair with all my youthful vitality ; creating new duties for myself, throwing out fresh feelers everywhere ; now and then crying out in my undisciplined way that the task was too hard for me ; that I loathed my life ; that it was impossible to live any longer without love and appreciation and sympathy ; that so uncongenial an atmosphere could be no home to me ; that the world was an utter negation and a mockery.

That was before I went to the hospital, at the time when my trouble was fresh and I was breaking my heart with the longing to see Charlie's face again. Most people who have lived long in the world, and have parted with their beloved, know what that sort of hopeless ache means.

My work was over at the hospital, and I had come home again to rest—so they said, but in reality to work out plans for my future life, in a sort of sullen silence, that seemed to shut me out from all sympathy.

It had wrapped me in a sort of mantle of reserve all the afternoon, during which I had been driving with Aunt Philippa and Sara. The air would do me good. I was moped, hipped, with all that dreary hospital work—so they said. It would distract and amuse me to watch Sara making her purchases. Reluctance, silent opposition, only whetted their charitable mood.

'Don't be disagreeable, Ursula. You might as well help me choose my new mantle,' Sara had said, quite pleasantly, and I had given in with a bad grace.

Another time I might have been amused

by Aunt Philippa's majestic deportment and
Sara's brisk importance, her girlish airs and
graces ; but I was too sad at heart to indulge
in my usual satire. Everything seemed stupid
and tiresome ; the hum of voices wearied me ;
the show-room at Marshall and Snelgrove's
seemed a confused Babel ; everywhere strange
voices—a hubbub of sound ; tall figures in
black passing and repassing ; strange faces reflected in endless pier-glasses—faces of puckered
anxiety repeating themselves in ludicrous *vrai-
semblance.*

I saw our own little group reproduced in
one. There was Aunt Philippa, tall and portly,
with her well-preserved beauty, a little full-
blown perhaps, but still ' marvellously ' good-
looking for her age, if she could only have not
been so conscious of the fact.

Then, Sara, standing there slim and
straight, with the furred mantle just slipping
over her smooth shoulders, radiant with good
health, good looks, perfectly contented with herself and the whole world, as it behoves a handsome, high-spirited young woman to be with
her surroundings, looking bright, unconcerned,
good-humoured, in spite of her mother's fussy

criticisms—Aunt Philippa was always a little fussy about dress.

Between the two I could just catch a glimpse of myself—a tall girl, dressed very plainly in black, with a dark complexion, large, anxious-looking eyes, that seemed appealing for relief from all this dulness—a shadowy sort of image of discontent and protest in the background, hovering behind Aunt Philippa's velvet mantle and Sara's slim, supple figure.

' Well, Ursula,' said Sara, still good-humouredly, ' will you not give us your opinion ? Does this dolman suit me, or would you prefer a long jacket trimmed with skunk ? '

I remember I decided in favour of the jacket, only Aunt Philippa interposed, a little contemptuously—

' What does Ursula know about the present fashion ? She has spent the last year in the wards of St. Thomas's, my dear,' dropping her voice, and taking up her gold-rimmed eyeglasses to inspect me more critically—a mere habit, for I had reason to know Aunt Philippa was not the least near-sighted. 'I cannot see any occasion for you to dress so dowdily, with three hundred a year to spend absolutely on yourself—for of course poor Charlie's little share has come to you. You could surely make yourself presentable, especially as you know we are going to Hyde Park Mansions to see Lesbia.'

This was too much for my equanimity. 'What does it matter? I am not coming with you, Aunt Philippa,' I retorted, somewhat vexed at this personality; but Sara overheard us and strove to pour oil on the troubled waters.

'Leave Ursula alone, mother; she looks tolerably well this afternoon; only mourning never suits a dark complexion—' But I did not wait to hear any more. I wandered about the place disconsolately, pretending to examine things with passing curiosity, but my eyes were throbbing and my heart beating angrily at Sara's thoughtless speech. A sudden remembrance seemed to steal before me vividly— Charlie's pale face, with its sad, sweet smile, haunted me. 'Courage, Ursula; it will be over soon.' Those were his last words, poor boy, and he was looking at me and not at Lesbia as he spoke. I always wondered what he meant by them. Was it his long pain, which he had borne so patiently, that would soon be over? or was it that cruel parting to which he alluded? or did he strive to comfort me at the last, with the assurance—alas! for our mortal nature, so sadly true—that pain cannot last for ever, that even faithful sorrow is shortlived and comforts itself in time; that I was young enough to outlive more than one trouble, and that I might take courage from this thought?

I looked down at the black dress, such as I had worn nearly two years for him, and raged as I remembered Sara's flippant words. 'My darling, I would wear mourning for you all my life gladly,' I said, with an inward sob that was more anger than sorrow, 'if I thought you would care for me to do it. Oh, what a world this is, Charlie, surely vanity and vexation of spirit!'

I did not mean to be cross with Sara, but my thoughts had taken a gloomy turn, and I could not recover my spirits—indeed, as we drove down Bond Street, where Sara had some glittering little toy to purchase, I reiterated my intention of not calling at Hyde Park Mansions.

'I do not want any tea,' I said wearily, ' and I would rather go home. Give my love to Lesbia; I will see her another day.'

'Lesbia will be hurt,' remonstrated Sara. 'What a little misanthrope you are, Ursula! St. Thomas's has injured you socially; you have become a hermit-crab all at once, and it is such nonsense at your age.'

'Oh, let me be, Sara!' I pleaded; 'I am tired, and Lesbia always chatters so; and Mrs. Fullerton is worse; besides, did you not tell me she was coming to dine with us this evening?'

'Yes, to be sure; but she wanted us to meet the Percy Glyns. Mirrel and Winifred Glyn are to be there this afternoon. Never mind, Lesbia will understand when I say you are in one of your ridiculous moods,' and Sara hummed a little tune gaily, as though she meant no offence by her words and was disposed to let me go my own way.

'The carriage can take you home, Ursula; we can walk those few yards,' observed Aunt Philippa as she descended leisurely and Sara tripped after her, still humming; but I took no notice of her words: I had had enough dulness

and decorum to last me for some time, the
Black Prince and his consort Bay might find
their way to their own stables without deposit-
ing me at the front door of the house at
Hyde Park Gate. I told Clarence so, to his
great astonishment, and walked across the road
in an opposite direction to home, as though my
feet were winged with quicksilver.

For the Park in that dim November light
seemed to allure me—there was a red glow of
sunset in the distance ; a faint, climbing mist
between the trees ; the gas-lamps were twinkling everywhere. I could hear the ringing of
some church bell ; there was space, freedom for
thought, a vague, uncertain prospect, out of
which figures were looming curiously ; a delightful sense that I was sinning against conventionality and Aunt Philippa.

'Halloa, Ursula !' exclaimed a voice in great
astonishment ; and there, out of the mist, was
a kind face looking at me—a face with a brown
beard, and dark eyes with a touch of amusement
in them ; and the eyes and the beard and the
bright, welcoming smile belonged to Uncle
Max.

As I caught at his outstretched hand with

a half-stifled exclamation of delight, a police-
man turned round and looked at us with an air
of interest. No doubt he thought the tall,
brown-bearded clergyman in the shabby coat—
it was one of Uncle Max's peculiarities to wear
a shabby coat occasionally—was the sweetheart
of the young lady in black. Uncle Max—I
am afraid I oftener called him Max—was only
a few years older than myself, and had occupied
the position of an elder brother to me.

He was my poor mother's only brother, and
had been dearly loved by her—not as I had
loved Charlie, perhaps ; but they had been
much to each other, and he had always seemed
nearer to me than Aunt Philippa, who was my
father's sister ; perhaps because there was
nothing in common between us, and I had
always been devoted to Uncle Max.

' Well, Ursula,' he said, pretending to
look grave, but evidently far too pleased to
see me to give me a very severe lecture,
' what is the meaning of this ?   Does Mrs.
Garston allow young ladies under her charge
to stroll about Hyde Park in the twilight, or
have you stolen a march on her—naughty little
she-bear ? '

I drew my hand away with an offended
air ; when Uncle Max wished to tease or punish
me he always reminded me that the name of
Ursula signified she-bear, and would sometimes
call me ' the little black growler ' ; and at such
times it was provoking to think that Sara signified Princess. I have always wondered how
far and how strongly our baptismal names influence us. Of course he would not let me
walk beside him in that dignified manner ;
the next instant I heard his clear hearty
laugh, and then I laughed too.

' What an absurd child you are ! I was
thinking over your letter as I walked along.
It did not bring me to London, certainly ; I
had business of my own ; but, all the same,
I have walked across the Park this evening to
talk to you about this extraordinary scheme.'

But I would not let him go on. He was
about to cross the road, so I took his arm
and turned him back. And there was the grey
mist creeping up between the trees, and the
lamps glimmering in the distance, and the faint
pink glow had not yet died away.

' It is so quiet here,' I pleaded, ' and I could
not get you alone for a moment if we went in.

Uncle Brian will be there, and Jill, and we could not say a word. Aunt Philippa and Sara have gone to see Lesbia. I have been driving with them all the afternoon. Sara has been shopping, and how bored I was!'

'You uncivilised little heathen!' Then, very gravely, 'Well, how is poor Lesbia?'

'Do not waste your pity on her,' I returned impatiently. 'She is as well and cheerful as possible. Even Sara says so. She is not breaking her heart about Charlie. She has left off mourning and is as gay as ever.'

'You are always hard on Lesbia,' he returned gently. 'She is young, my dear, you forget that, and a pretty girl, and very much admired. It always seems to me she was very fond of the poor fellow.'

'She was good to him in his illness, but she never cared for Charlie as he did for her. He worshipped the very ground she walked on. He thought her perfection. Uncle Max, it was pitiful to hear him sometimes. He would tell me how sweet and unselfish she was, and all the time I knew she was but an ordinary, commonplace girl. If he had lived to marry her he would have been disappointed in her. He was so large-hearted, and Lesbia has such little aims.'

'So you always say, Ursula. But you women are so severe in your judgment of each other. I doubt myself if the girl lives whom you would have considered good enough for Charlie. Yes, yes, my dear'—as I uttered a dissenting protest to this—' he was a fine fellow, and his was a most lovable character; but it was his last illness that ripened him.'

'He was always perfect in my eyes,' I returned, in a choked voice.

'That was because you loved him; and no doubt Lesbia possessed the same ideal goodness for him. Love throws its own glamour,' he went on, and his voice was unusually grave; ' it does not believe in commonplace mediocrity; it lifts up its idol to some fanciful pedestal, where the poor thing feels very uncomfortable and out of its element, and then persists in falling down and worshipping it. We humans are very droll, Ursula; we will create our own divinities.'

'Lesbia would have disappointed him,' I persisted, obstinately; but I might as well have talked to the wind. Uncle Max could not

find it in his heart to be hard to a pretty
girl.

'That is open to doubt, my dear. Lesbia
is amiable and charming, and I daresay she
would have made a nice little wife. Poor Charlie
hated clever women, and in that respect she
would have suited him.'

After this I knew it was no good in trying
to change his opinion. Uncle Max held his
own views with remarkable tenacity; he had
old-fashioned notions with respect to women,
rather singular in so young a man—for he was
only thirty; he preferred to believe in their
goodness, in spite of any amount of demonstra-
tion to the contrary; it vexed him to be reminded of the shortcomings of his friends;
by nature he was an optimist, and had a large
amount of faith in people's good intentions.
'He meant well, poor fellow, in spite of his
failures,' was a speech I have heard more than
once from his lips. He was always ready to
condone a fault or heal a breach; indeed, his
sweet nature found it difficult to bear a grudge
against any one; he was only hard to himself,
and on no one else did he strive to impose so
heavy a yoke. I was only silent for a minute,

and then I turned the conversation into another channel.

'But my letter, Uncle Max!'

'Ah, true, your letter ; but I have not forgotten it. How old are you, Ursula? I always forget.'

'Five-and-twenty this month.'

'To be sure—I ought to have remembered ; and you have three hundred a year of your own.'

I nodded.

'And your present home is distasteful to you?' in an inquiring tone.

'It is no home to me,' I returned passionately. 'Oh, Uncle Max, how can one call it home after the dear old rectory, where we were so happy, father, and mother, and Charlie— and——'

'Yes, I know, poor child ; and you have had heavy troubles. It cannot be like the old home, I am well aware of that, Ursula ; but your aunt is a good woman. I have always found her strictly just. She was your father's only sister ; when she offered you a home she promised to treat you with every indulgence, as though you were her own daughter.'

'Aunt Philippa means to be kind,' I said, struggling to repress my tears—tears always troubled Uncle Max—'she is kind in her way, and so is Sara. I have every comfort, every luxury; they want me to be gay and enjoy myself, to lead their life; but it only makes me miserable; they do not understand me; they see I do not think with them, and then they laugh at me and call me morbid. No one really wants me but poor Jill—I am so fond of Jill.'

'Why cannot you lead their life, Ursula?'

'Because it is not life at all,' was my resolute answer; 'to me it is the most wearisome existence possible. Listen to me, Uncle Max. Do you think I could possibly spend my days as Sara does—writing a few notes, doing a little fancy work, shopping and paying visits, and dancing half the night? Do you think you could transform such a poor little Cinderella into a fairy princess, like Sara, or Lesbia? No; the drudgery of such a life would kill me with *ennui* and discontent.'

'It is not the life I would choose for you, certainly,' he said, pulling his beard in some perplexity; 'it is far too worldly to suit my taste; if Charlie had lived you would have made your home with him. He often talked to me about that, poor fellow. I thought a year or two at Hyde Park Gate would do you no harm, and might be wholesome training; but it has proved a failure, I see that.'

'They would be happier without me,' I went on more quietly, for he was evidently coming round to my view of the case. 'Aunt Philippa does not mean to be unkind, but she often lets me see that I am in the way, that she is not proud of me. She would have taken more interest in me if I had been handsome, like Sara; but a plain, dowdy niece is not to her taste. No, let me finish, Uncle Max'—for he wanted to interrupt me here. 'They made a great fuss about my training at the hospital last year, but I am sure they did not miss me; Sara spoke yesterday as though she thought I was going back to St. Thomas's, and Aunt Philippa made no objection. I heard her tell Mrs. Fullerton once "that really Ursula was so strong-minded and different from other girls that she was prepared for anything, even for her being a female doctor."'

'Well, my dear, you are certainly rather peculiar, you know.'

'Oh, Uncle Max,' I said mournfully, ' are you going to misunderstand me too ? Providence has deprived me of my parents and my only brother ; is it strong-minded or peculiar to be so lonely and sad at heart that gaiety only jars on me ? Can I forget my mother's teaching, when she said, "Ursula, if you live for the world you will be miserable. Try to do your duty and benefit your fellow-creatures, and happiness must follow " ? '

' Yes, poor Emmie, she was a good woman : you might do worse than take after her.'

' She would not approve of the life I am leading at Hyde Park Gate,' I went on. ' She and Aunt Philippa never cared for each other. I often think that if she had known she would not have liked me to be there. Sundays are wretched. We go to church ?—yes, because it is respectable to do so ; but there is a sort of re-union every Sunday evening.'

' I wish I could offer you a home, Ursula ; but——' here Uncle Max hesitated.

' That would not do at all,' I returned promptly ; ' your bachelor home would not do for me ; besides, you might marry—of course, you will,' but he flushed rather uncomfortably

at that, and said, ' Pshaw ! what nonsense !' We
had paused under a lamp-post, and I could see
him plainly ; perhaps he knew this, for he hurried me on, this time in the direction of home.

'I am five-and-twenty,' I continued, trying
to collect the salient points of my argument. ' I
am indebted to none for my maintenance ; I am
free, and my own mistress ; I neglect no duty
by refusing to live under Uncle Brian's roof;
no one wants me ; I contribute to no one's
happiness.'

' Except to Jill's,' observed Uncle Max.

' Jill ! but she is only a child, barely sixteen,
and Sara is becoming jealous of my influence.
I shall only breed dissension in the household
if I remain. Uncle Max, you are a good man
—a clergyman—you cannot conscientiously
tell me that I am not free to lead my own life,
to choose my own work in the world.'

' Perhaps not,' he replied, in a hesitating
voice. ' But the scheme is a peculiar one. You
wish me to find respectable lodgings in my
parish, where you will be independent and free
from supervision, and to place your superfluous
health and strength—you are a muscular
Christian, Ursula—at the service of my sick

poor, and for this post you have previously
trained yourself.'

I think it will be a good sort of life,' I
returned carelessly, but how my heart was
beating! 'I like it so much, and I should like
to be near you, Uncle Max, and work under
you as my vicar. I have thought about this for
years. Charlie and I often talked of it. I was
to live with him and Lesbia, and devote my
time to this work. He thought it such a nice
idea to go and nurse poor people in their homes.
And he promised that he would come and sing
to them. But now I must carry out my plan
alone, for Charlie cannot help me now.' And
as I thought of the sympathy that had never
failed me my voice quivered and I could say
no more.

'I wish we were all in heaven,' growled
Uncle Max—but his tone was a little husky—
'for this world is a most uncomfortable place
for good people, or people with a craze. I
think Charlie is well out of it.'

'Under which category do you mean to
place me?' I asked, trying to laugh.

'My dear, there is a craze in most women.
They have such an obstinate faith in their

own good intentions. If they find half a dozen fools to believe in them they will start a crusade to found a new Utopia. Women are the most meddlesome things in creation : they never let well alone. Their pretty little fingers are in every human pie. That is why we get so much unwholesome crust and so little meat, and, of course, our digestion is ruined.'

'Uncle Max '——— but he would not be serious any longer.

'Ursula, I utterly refuse to inhale any more of this mist. I think a comfortable armchair by the fire would be far more conducive to comfort. You have given me plenty of food for thought, and I mean to sleep on it. Now, not another word. I am going to ring the bell.' And Uncle Max was as good as his word.

CHAPTER II.

BEHIND THE BARS.

IT was quite true, as I had told Uncle Max, that the scheme had been no new one; it was no sudden emanation from a girl's brain, morbid with discontent and fruitless longings; it had grown with my youth and had become part of my environment. As a child the thought had come to me, as I followed my father into one cottage after another in his house-to-house visitation. He had been a conscientious, hard-working clergyman; in fact, his work killed him, for he overtasked a constitution that was not naturally strong. I accompanied my mother too in her errands of mercy, and saw a great deal of the misery engendered by drink, ignorance, and want of forethought. In the case of the sick poor, the gross mis-

management and want of cleanly and thrifty
habits led to an amount of discomfort and
suffering that even now makes me shudder. The
parish was overgrown and insufficiently worked ;
the greater part of the population belonged to
the working classes ; dissenting chapels and gin-
palaces flourished. Often did my childish heart
ache at the surroundings of some squalid home,
where the parents toiled all day for worse than
nought, just to satisfy their unhealthy cravings,
while the children grew up riotous, half starved,
and full of inherited vices.   There was a little
child I saw once, a cripple, dying slowly of
some sad spinal disease, lying in a dark corner,
on what seemed to me a heap of rags. O God,
I can see that child's face now ! I remember
when we heard of its death my mother burst
into tears. They were tears of joy, she told me
afterwards, that another suffering child's life
was ended, ' and there are hundreds and hundreds of these little creatures, Ursula,' she said,
' growing up in sin and misery ; and the world
goes on, and people eat and drink and are
merry, for it is none of their business, and yet
it is not the will of the Father that one of these
little ones should perish.'

I had learned much from my father, but still more from my mother. Uncle Max had called her a good woman, but she was more than that : she possessed one of those rare unselfish natures that cannot remain satisfied with their own personal happiness: they wish to include the whole world. She wanted to inculcate in me her own spirit of self-sacrifice. I can remember some of her short, trenchant sentences now.

'Never mind happiness : that is God's gift to a few—do your duty.'

'If you have loved your fellow-creatures sufficiently you will not be afraid to die. A good conscience will smooth your pillow.'

And once, in her last illness, when Charlie asked if she were comfortable, 'Not very, but I shall soon be quite comfortable, for I shall hope to forget in heaven how little I have done after all, here ; and yet I always wanted to help others.'

Oh, how good she was ! And Charlie was good too, after the fashion of young men : not altogether thoughtless, full of the promptings of his kind heart ; but Uncle Max was right when he said his last illness had ripened him :

it was not the old careless Charlie who had
wooed Lesbia who lay there : it was another
and better Charlie.

In the old days he had rallied me in a
brotherly manner on my old-fashioned, grave
ways. 'You are not a modern young lady,
Ursie,' he would say ; and he would often call
me ' grandmother Ursula ; ' but all the same
he would listen to my plans with the utmost
tolerance and good-nature.

Ah, those talks in the twilight, before the
fatal disease developed itself, and he lay in idle
fashion on the couch with his arms under his
head, while I sat on the foot-stool or on the
rug in the firelight ! We were to live together
—yes, that was always the dream ; even when
Lesbia's fair face came between us he would
not hear of any difference. I was to live with
him and Lesbia. Lesbia was rich, and though
Charlie had little, they were to marry soon.

I was to form a part of that luxurious
household, but my time was to be my own, and
I was to devote it to the sick poor of Rutherford. ' Mind, Ursula, you may work, but I will
not have you overwork,' Charlie had once said,
more decidedly than usual; ' you must come

home for hours of rest and refreshment. You
have a beautiful voice, and it shall be properly
trained ; you may sing to your invalids as much
as you like, and sometimes I will come and
sing too ; but you must remember you have
social duties, and I shall expect you to entertain our friends.' And it was the idea of this
dual life of home sympathy and outside work
that had so strongly seized upon my imagination.

When Charlie died I was too sick at heart
to carry out my plan. 'How can one work
alone ? ' I would say sorrowfully to myself ; but
after a time the emptiness of my life and dis-
satisfaction with my surroundings brought back
the old thoughts.

I remembered the dear old rectory life,
where every one was in earnest, and contrasted it with the trifling pursuits that my
aunt and cousin called duties. My present
existence seemed to shut me in like prison bars.
Only to be free, to choose my own life ! And then
came emancipation in the shape of hard hospital work, when health and spirits returned to
me ; when, under the stimulus of useful employ-
ment and constant exercise of body and mind,

I slept better, fretted less, and looked less mournfully out on the world. Uncle Max was right when he said a year at St. Thomas's would save me.

By-and-by the idea dawned upon me that I might still carry out my plan; there were poor people at Heathfield, where Uncle Max's parish was. What should hinder me from living there under Uncle Max's wing and trying to combine the two lives, as Charlie wished?

I was young, full of activity. I did not wish to shut myself out from my kind. I could discharge my duties to my own class and enjoy a moderate amount of pleasure. I was young enough to desire that; but the greater part of my time would be placed at the disposal of my poorer neighbours. People might think it singular at first, but they would not talk for ever, and the life would be a happy one to me.

All this had been said in that voluminous letter of mine to Uncle Max; he might argue and shake his head over it, thereby proving himself a wise man; but he could not but know that I was absolutely under my own control, as far as a woman could be. I need ask no one's advice in the disposal of my own life; his own and Uncle Brian's guardianship was merely nominal now. After five-and-twenty I was declared my own mistress in every sense of the word.

Uncle Brian came out to meet us as soon as he heard Uncle Max's voice in the hall; the two were very great friends, and they shook hands cordially.

'Glad to see you, Cunliffe; why did you not let us know that you were coming up to town? We could have put you up easily—eh, Ursula?'

'Yes, indeed, Uncle Brian;' and then I added coaxingly, 'Do please send for your portmanteau, Uncle Max; you know Lesbia is coming this evening, and you are such a favourite with her.' I knew this would be a strong inducement, for Uncle Max's soft heart would insist on treating Lesbia as though she were a widowed princess.

'All right,' he returned in his lazy way, and then I took the matter into my own hands by leaving the room at once to consult with Mrs. Martin—Aunt Philippa's housekeeper.

As I closed the door I glanced back for another look at Uncle Max. He had thrown himself into an easy-chair, as though he were tired, and was leaning back with his hands under his head in Charlie's fashion, looking up at Uncle Brian, who was standing on the rug.

I always thought Uncle Brian a very handsome man. He had clear, well-cut features, and a grey moustache, and he was quiet and dignified. He always looked to me, with his brown complexion, more like an Indian officer than a wealthy banker. There was nothing commercial in his appearance; but I should have admired him more if he had been less cold and repressive in manner; but he was an undemonstrative man, even to his own children.

I remember hinting this once to Uncle Max, and he had rebuked me more severely than he had ever done before.

'I do not like young girls like you, Ursula, to be so critical about their elders. Garston is an excellent fellow; he has plenty of brains, and always does the right thing, however difficult it may be. Men are not like women, my dear—they often hide their deepest feelings. Your poor uncle has never been quite the same man since Ralph's death, and just as he was getting over his boy's loss a little he had a fresh disappointment with Charlie; he always meant to put him in Ralph's place.'

I was a little ashamed of my criticism when Max said this. I felt I had not made sufficient allowance for Uncle Brian: the death of his only son must have been a dreadful blow. Ralph had died at Oxford; they said he had overworked himself in trying for honours and then had taken a chill. He was a fine, handsome young fellow, nearly two-and-twenty, and his father's idol: no wonder Uncle Brian had grown so much older and graver during the last few years.

And he had been fond of Charlie, and had meant to have him in Ralph's place; my poor boy would have been a rich one if he had lived. Uncle Brian had taken him into the bank, and Lesbia and her fortune were promised to him, but the goodly heritage was snatched away before his eyes, and he was called away in the fresh bloom of his youth.

I always thought Uncle Brian liked Max better than any other man—he was always less stiff and frigid in his presence. I could hear his

low laugh—Uncle Brian never laughed loudly
—as I closed the door; Max had said something
that amused him. They would be quite happy
without me, so I ran up to the schoolroom on
the chance of getting a chat with Jill.

The schoolroom was on the second floor,
where Jill, I, and Fräulein all slept. Sara had
a handsome room next to her mother's, and a
little boudoir furnished most daintily for her
special use. I do not believe she ever sat in it,
unless she had a cold or was otherwise ailing;
the drawing-room was always full of company,
and Sara was the life of the house. I used to
peep in at the pretty room sometimes as I went
up to bed; there were few notes written at the
inlaid escritoire, the handsomely-bound books
were never taken down from the shelves.
Draper, Aunt Philippa's maid, fed the canaries
and dusted the cabinets of china. Sometimes
Sara would trip into the room with one of her
cronies for a special chat; the ripple of their
girlish laughter would reach us as Jill and I sat
together. 'Whom has Sara got with her this
afternoon?' Jill would say peevishly. 'Do listen
to them; they do nothing but laugh; if
Fräulein had set her all these exercises she

would not feel quite so merry,' Jill would
finish, throwing the obnoxious book from her
with a little burst of impatience.

I always pitied Jill for having to spend her
days in such a dull room; the furniture was
ugly, and the windows looked out on a dismal
backyard, with the high walls of the opposite
building. Aunt Philippa, who was a rigid dis-
ciplinarian with her young daughter, always
said that she had chosen the room 'because Jill
would have nothing to distract her from her
studies.' The poor child would put up her
shoulders at this remark and draw down the
corners of her lips in a way that would make
Aunt Philippa scold her for her awkwardness.
'You need not make yourself plainer than you
are, Jocelyn,' she would say severely; for Jill's
awkward manners troubled her motherly vanity.
'What is the good of all the dancing and drill-
ing and riding with Captain Cooper if you will
persist in hunching your shoulders as though
you were deformed. Fräulein has been com-
plaining of you this morning; she seems excessively displeased at your carelessness and
want of application.' 'I know I shall get stupid,
shut up in that dull hole with Fräulein,' Jill

would say passionately, after one of these maternal lectures. Aunt Philippa was really very fond of Jill; but she misunderstood the girl's nature. The system had answered so well with Sara, that she could not be brought to comprehend why it should fail with her other child. Sara had grown up blooming and radiant in spite of the depressing influences of Fräulein and the dull narrow schoolroom. Her music and singing masters had come to her there. Little Madame Blanchard had chirped to her in Parisian accent for the hour together over *les modes* and *le beau Paris*. Sara had danced and drilled with the other young ladies at Miss Dugald's select establishment, and had joined them at the riding school or in the cavalcade under Captain Cooper.

Sara had worn her bondage lightly, and had fascinated even grim old Herr Schliefer. Her tact and easy adaptability had kept Fräulein Sonnenschein in a state of tepid good humour; every one, even cross old Draper, idolised Sara for her beauty and sprightly ways. When Aunt Philippa declared her education finished she tripped out of the schoolroom as happily as possible, to take possession of her grand new bedroom and the little boudoir, where all her girlish treasures were arranged. She had not been the least impatient for her day of freedom ; it would all come in good time. When the sceptre was put into her hands and her sovereignty acknowledged by the whole household, the young princess was not a bit excited. She put on her Court dress and made her curtsey to her Majesty with the same charming unconsciousness and ease of manner. No wonder people were charmed with such good humour and freshness. If the glossy hair did not cover a large amount of brains, no one found fault with her for that.

Jill raged and stormed fiercely under Sara's light-hearted philosophy ; when her sister told her to be patient under Fräulein's yoke, that a good time was coming for her also, when lesson books would be shut up, and Herr Schliefer would cease to scatter snuff on the carpet as he sat drumming with his fingers on the keyboard and grunting out brief interjections of impatience.

'What does it matter about Herr Schliefer,' Jill would say in a sort of fury. 'I like him a hundred times better than I do that mincing little poll-parrot of a Madame Blanchard : she is odious, and I hate her, and I hate Fräulein too. It is not the lessons I mind ; one has to learn lessons all one's life ; it is being shut up like a bird in a cage when one's wings are ready for flight. I should like to fly away from this room, from Fräulein, from the whole of the horrid set ; it makes me cross, wicked, to live like this, and all your sugar-plums will do me no good. Go away, Sara ; you do not understand as Ursula does. It makes me feel bad to see you standing there, looking so pretty and happy, and just laughing at me.'

'Of course I laugh at you, Jocelyn, when you behave like a baby,' returned Sara, trying to be severe, only her dimples betrayed her. 'Well, as you are so cross, I shall go away. There is the chocolate I promised you. Ta-ta.' And Sara put down the *bonbonnière* on the table and walked out of the room.

I was not surprised to see Jill push it away. No one understood the poor child but myself ; she was precocious, womanly, for her age ; she had twenty times the amount of brains that Sara possessed, and she was starving on the education provided for her.

To dance and drill and write dreary German exercises, when one is thirsting to drink deeply at the well of knowledge; to go round and round the narrow monotonous course that had sufficed for Sara's moderate abilities, like the blind horse at the mill, and never to advance an inch out of the beaten track—this was simply maddening to Jill's sturdy intellect. She often told me how she longed to attend classes, to hear lectures, to rub against full-grown minds.

'Now, Me-ess Jocelyn, we will do a little of ze Wallenstein, by the immortal Schiller. Hold up the head, and leave off striking the table with your elbows.' Jill would give a droll imitation of Fräulein, and end with a groan.

'What does she know about Schiller? She cannot even comprehend him. She is dense—utterly dense and stupid; but because she knows her own language and has a correct deportment she is fit to teach me.' And Jill ground her little white teeth in impotent wrath. Jill always appeared to me like an infant Pegasus in harness; she wanted to soar—to make use of her wings—and they kept her down. She was not naturally gay, like Sara, though her health was good, and she was as powerful as a young Amazon. Her nature was more sombre, and took colour from her surroundings.

She was like a child in the sunshine, plenty of life and movement distracted her from interior broodings and made her joyous; when she was riding with the young ladies from Miss Dugald's, she would be as merry as the others.

But her dreary schoolroom and Fräulein's society chafed her nervous sensibilities dangerously; there were only a few brown sparrows, or a stray cat intent on game, to be seen from her window. From the drawing-room, from Sara's boudoir, from her mother's bedroom, there was a charming view of the park. In the spring the fresh foliage of the trees, and the velvety softness of the grass, would be delicious; down in the broad white road, carriages were passing, horses cantering, happy-looking people in smart bonnets, in gorgeous mantles, driving about everywhere; children would be running up and down the paths in the park, flower-sellers would stand offering their innocent wares to the passengers. Jill would sit entranced by her mother's window watching them; the sunshine, the glitter, the hubbub intoxicated her; she made up stories by the dozen, as her dark eyes followed the gay equipages. When Fräulein summoned her she went away reluctantly; the stories got into her head, and stopped there all the time she laboured through that long sonata.

'Why are your fingers all thumbs to-day, Fräulein?' Herr Schliefer would demand gloomily. Jill, who was really fond of the stern old professor, hung her head and blushed guiltily. She had no excuse to offer, her girlish dreams were sacred to her, they came gliding to her through the most intricate passages of the sonata, now with a *staccato* movement— brisk, lively—with fitful energy, now *andante*, then *crescendo, con passione.* Jill's unformed girlish hands strike the chords wildly, angrily. '*Dolce, dolce,*' screams the professor in her ears; the music softens, wanes, and the dreams seem to die away too. 'That will do, Fräulein, you have not acquitted yourself so badly after all;' and Jill gets off her music-stool reluctant, absent, half-awake, and her day dream broken up into chaos.

CHAPTER III.

CINDERELLA.

S I opened the schoolroom door a half-forgotten picture of Cinderella came vividly before me.

The fire had burnt low, a heap of black ashes lay under the grate; and by the dull red glow I could see Jill's forlorn figure, very indistinctly, as she sat in her favourite attitude on the rug, her arms clasping her knees, and her short black locks hanging loosely over her shoulders. She gave a little shrill exclamation of pleasure when she saw me.

'Ah, you dear darling bear, do come and hug me,' she cried, trying to get up in a hurry, but her dress entangled her.

'Where is Fräulein?' I asked, pushing her back into her place, while I knelt down to manipulate the miserable fire. 'Jill, you look just like Cinderella, when the proud sisters drove away to the ball. My dear, were you asleep; why are you sitting in the dark, with the fire going out, and the lamp unlighted? There, it only wanted to be stirred ; we shall have light by which to see each other's faces directly.'

'Fräulein has a headache and has gone to lie down,' returned Jill, and though I could not see her clearly, I knew at once by her voice that she had been crying; only she would have been furious if I had noticed the fact. 'I hope I am not very wicked, but Fräulein's headaches are the redeeming points in her character; she has them so often, and then she is obliged to lie down.'

'Of course you have offered to bathe her head?' I asked a little mischievously, but Jill, who was unusually subdued, took the question in good part.

'Oh, yes, and I spoke to her quite civilly ; but I suppose she saw the savage gleam of delight in my eyes, for she was as cross as possible, and went away muttering that "Meess Jocelyn had the heart like the flint; if it had

been Meess Sara, now——" and then she banged
the door, so the pain could not have been so
bad after all. It is my belief,' went on Jill,
' that Fräulein always has a headache when she
has a novel to finish. Mamma does not like
her to set me an example of novel-reading, so
she is obliged to lock herself in her own room.'

I took no notice of this statement, as I
rather leaned to this view of the subject
myself. Fräulein's round placid face and excellent appetite showed no signs of suffering,
and her constant plea of a bad headache was
only received with any credulity by Aunt
Philippa herself; neither Sara nor I had much
respect for Fräulein Sonnenschein, with her
thick little figure, and big head covered with
flimsy flaxen plaits. We were both aware of
the smooth selfishness of her character, though
Sara chose to ignore it for Jill's benefit. She
was industrious, painstaking, and capable of a
great deal of dull routine in the way of duties,
but she was far too fond of her own comfort,
and all the affection of which she was capable
was lavished upon her own relatives; she had
cared for Sara moderately, but her other pupil,
Jill, was a thorn in her side. So I passed over

Fräulein's headache without comment, and took Jill to task somewhat sharply for the comfortless state of the room. A good scolding would rouse her from her dejection; the blinds were up and the curtains undrawn; the remains of a meal, the usual five o'clock schoolroom tea, was still on the table. Jill's German books were heaped up beside her empty cup and the glass dish that contained marmalade; the kettle spluttered and hissed in the blaze; Jill's little black kitten, Sooty, was dragging a half-knitted stocking across the rug.

'I forgot to ring for Martha,' faltered Jill; 'she will come presently. Don't be cross, Ursula. I like the room as it is; it is deliciously untidy, just like Cinderella's kitchen; but there is no hope of the fairy godmother; and you are going away, and I shall be ten times more miserable.'

It was this that was troubling her, then; for I had told her my plans and all about my letter to Uncle Max. Perhaps she had heard his voice in the hall, for Jill's pretty little ears heard everything that went on in the house; she admitted her knowledge at once when I taxed her with it.

'Oh yes, I know Mr. Cunliffe is here. I heard papa go out and speak to him ; his voice sounded quite cheerful ; and now he has come and it will all be settled ; and you will go away and be happy with your poor people, and forget that I am fretting myself to death in this horrid room.'

She had drawn me down on the rug forcibly—for she had the strength of a young Titaness—and was wrapping her arms round me with a sort of fierce impatience. Her big eyes looked troubled and affectionate. Few people admired Jill ; she was undeveloped and awkward, full of angles, and a little brusque in manner ; she had a way of thrusting out her big feet and squaring her shoulders that horrified Aunt Philippa. She was very big, certainly, and would never possess Sara's slim grace. Her hair had been cropped in some illness, and had not grown so fast as they expected, but hung in short thick lengths about her neck ; it was always getting into her eyes, and was being pushed back impatiently, but she would much oftener throw her head back with a fling like an unbroken pony, for she was jerky as young things often are.

But though people found fault with Jill, and often said that she would never be as handsome as Sara, I liked her face. Perhaps it was a little irregular and her complexion slightly sallow, but when she was flushed or excited and she opened her big bright eyes, and one could see her little white teeth gleaming as she laughed, I have thought Jill could look almost beautiful; but her good looks depended on her expression.

' I suppose it will be settled,' I replied, with a quick catch at my breath, for the mere mention of the subject excited me; ' but you will be a good child and not fret if I do go away. No, I shall never forget you,' as a close hug answered me, ' I love you too dearly for that ; but I want you to be brave about it, dear, for I cannot be happy wasting my time and doing nothing. You know how ill I was before I went to St. Thomas's, so that Uncle Max was obliged to tell Aunt Philippa that I must have change and hard work, or I should follow Charlie.'

' Oh yes, and we were all so frightened about you, you poor thing; you looked so pinched and miserable. Well, I suppose I must let you go, as you are so wicked as to disobey the proverb that " Charity begins at home." '

' Listen to me, dear,' I returned, quite pleased to find her so reasonable. 'I am very glad to know that I have been a comfort to you, but I shall hope to be so still. I will write long letters to you, Jill, and tell you all about my work, and you shall answer them, and talk to me on paper about the books you have read, and the queer thoughts you have, and how patient and strong you have grown, and how you have learnt to put up with Fräulein's little ways and not aggravate her with your untidiness.' And here Jill's hand, and it was by no means a small hand, closed my lips rather abruptly. But I was used to this sort of sledge-hammer form of argument.

' Oh, it is all very fine for you to sit there and moralise, Ursula, like a sort of sucking Diogenes,' grumbled Jill, ' when you know you are going to have your own way and live a deliciously sort of three-volume-novel life, not like any one else's, unless it were Don Quixote, or one of the Knights of the Round Table, poking about among a lot of strange people, doing wonderful things for them, until they are all ready to worship you. It is all very well for you, I say, but what would you do if you were me,' cried Jill, in her shrill treble, and quite oblivious of grammatical niceties ; 'how would you like to be poor me, shut up here with that old dragon ? '

This was a grand opportunity for airing my philosophy, and I rushed at it. To Jill's amazement, I shook my hair back in the way she usually shook her rough black mane, and opening my eyes very widely, tried to copy Jill's falsetto.

'How thankful I am Jocelyn Garston and not Ursula Garston,' I said, with rapid staccato. 'Poor Ursula! I am fond of her, but I would not change places with her for the world. She has known such a lot of trouble in her life, more than most girls, I believe ; she has lost her lovely home—such a sweet old place—and her mother and father and Charlie, all her nearest and her most beloved, and she is so sad that she wants to work hard and forget her troubles.'

' Oh dear,' sighed Jill at this.

'How happy I am compared with her,' I

went on, relapsing unconsciously into my own
voice. 'I am young and strong; I have all my
life before me ; true, poor Ralph has gone, but
I was only a child and did not miss him. I
have a good father and an indulgent mother
('Humph,' observed Jill at this point, only she
turned it into a cough); if my present schoolroom life is not to my taste, I am sensible
enough to know that the drudgery and re-
straint will not last for long; in another year,
or a year and a half, Fräulein, whom I certainly
do not love, will go back to her own country.
I shall be free to read the books I like ; to
study what I choose; or to be idle. I shall
have Sara's cheerful companionship instead of
Fräulein's heavy company. I shall ride ; I shall
walk in the sunshine ; I shall be a butterfly instead of a chrysalis ; and if I care to be useful,
all sorts of paths will be open to me.'

'There, hold your tongue,' interrupted Jill,
with a rough kiss; ' of course I know I am a
wicked, ungrateful wretch, and that I ought to
be more patient. Yes, you shall go, Ursula ;
you are a darling ; but I will not want to keep
you ; you are too good to be wasted on me ;
it would be like pouring gold into a sieve ;

well, I did cry about it this afternoon, but I won't be such a goose any more. I will live my life the same day, in spite of all of them, you will see if I don't, Ursula; who is it who says, " The thoughts of youth are long, long thoughts "? I have such big thoughts sometimes, especially when I sit in the dark. I send them out like strange birds, all over the world —up, up, everywhere, but they never come back to me again,' finished Jill, mournfully ; ' if they build nests I never know it; I just sit and puzzle out things like poor little grimy Cinderella.'

Jill's eloquence did not surprise me. I knew she was very clever, and full of un-fledged poetry, and I had often heard her talk in that way ; but I had no time to answer her, for just then the first gong sounded, and I could hear Sara running up to her room to dress for dinner. Jill jumped up, and tugged at the bell-rope rather fiercely.

'Martha must have forgotten all about the tea-things ; very likely the lamp is smoky and will have to be trimmed. I must not come and help you, Ursie, dear, for I have to learn my German poetry before I dress.' And Jill pulled down the blinds and drew the curtains with a vigorous hand. Martha looked quite frightened at the sight of Jill's energy and her own re-missness.

'Why did you not ring before, Miss Jocelyn?' she said plaintively, and in rather an injured voice, as she carried away the tea-tray.

Uncle Max passed me in the passage; Clarence was following with his portmanteau; he looked surprised to see me still in my bonnet with my fur cape trailing over one arm; but I nodded to him cheerfully and went quickly into my room.

My life at St. Thomas's had inured me to hardness; it had contrasted strangely with my luxurious surroundings at Hyde Park Gate. Aunt Philippa certainly treated me well in her way. I had a full share of the loaves and fishes of the household; my room was as prettily furnished as Jill's; a bright fire burnt in the grate; there were pink candles on the dressing-table. Martha, who waited upon us both, had put out my black evening dress on the bed, and had warmed my dressing-gown; she would come to me by-and-by with a civil offer of help.

I was rather puzzled at the sight of a little breast-knot of white chrysanthemums that lay on the table, until I remembered Uncle Max; no one had ever brought me flowers since Charlie's death; he had gathered the last that I ever wore: some white violets that grew in a little hollow in the ground of Rutherford Lodge. I hesitated painfully before I pinned the modest little bouquet in my black dress, but I feared Uncle Max would be hurt if I failed to appear in it. I wore mother's pearl necklace as usual, and the little locket with her hair; somehow I took more pleasure in dressing myself this evening, when I knew Uncle Max's kind eyes would be on me.

I had not hurried myself, and the second gong sounded before I reached the drawing-room, so I came face to face with Lesbia who was coming out on Uncle Brian's arm. She kissed me in her quiet way, and said, 'How do you do, Ursula?' just as though we had met yesterday, and passed on.

I thought she looked prettier than ever that evening—like a snow princess, in her white gown, with a little fleecy shawl drawn round her shoulders, for she took cold easily. She had a soft creamy complexion, and fair hair that she wore piled up in smooth plaits on her head; she had plaintive blue eyes that could be brilliant at times, and a lovely mouth, and she was tall and graceful like Sara.

They made splendid foils to each other; but in my opinion Sara carried the palm: she was more piquant and animated; her colouring was brighter, and she had more expression; but Charlie's Lily, as he called her, was quite as much admired, and indeed they were both striking-looking girls.

I saw that Uncle Max took a great deal of notice of Lesbia, who sat next to him. I could not hear their conversation, but a pretty pink colour tinged Lesbia's face, and her eyes grew dark and bright as she listened, and I saw her glance at her left hand where the half-hoop of diamonds still glistened that Charlie had placed there; she had not quite forgotten the dear boy then, for I am sure she sighed, but the next moment she had turned from Uncle Max, and was engaged in an eager discussion with Sara, about some private theatricals in which Sara was to take a part.

When we went back to the drawing-room

we found Fräulein in her favourite red silk
dress, trying to repair the damage that Sooty
had wrought in her half-knitted stocking, and
Jill, looking very bored and uncomfortable,
turning over the photograph album in a
corner. She looked awkward and sallow in
her Indian muslin gown—the flimsy stuff did
not suit her any more than the pink coral
beads she wore round her neck. Her black
locks bobbed uneasily over the book. She
looked bigger than ever when she stood up to
speak to Lesbia.

'How that child is growing,' observed Aunt
Philippa behind her fan to Fräulein, whose
round face was beaming with smiles at the
entrance of the ladies. 'That gown was made
only a few weeks ago, and she is growing out
of it already. Jocelyn, my love, why do you
hunch your shoulders so when you talk to
Lesbia? I am always telling you of this awkward habit.'

Poor Jill frowned and reddened a little
under this maternal admonition; her eyes looked
black and fierce as she sat down again with her
photographs. This hour was always a penance
to her; she could not speak or move easily

for fear of some remark from Aunt Philippa.
When her mother and Fräulein interchanged
confidences behind that big spangled fan, the
poor child always thought they were talking
about her.

Her bigness, her awkwardness, troubled Jill
excessively. Her clumsy hands and feet seemed
always in her way.

'I know I am the ugly duckling,' she
would say, with tears in her eyes; 'but I shall
never turn into a swan like Sara and Lesbia—
not that I want to be like them!'—with a little
scorn in her voice. 'Lesbia is too tame—too
namby-pamby for my taste; and Sara is
stupid. She laughs and talks, but she never
says anything that people have not said a hundred times before. Oh! I am so tired of it all.
I grow more cross and disagreeable every day,'
finished Jill, who was very frank on the subject of her shortcoming.

I would have stopped and talked to Jill,
only Lesbia tapped me on the arm rather peremptorily—

'Come into the back drawing-room,' she
said in a low voice, 'I want to speak to you.
Jill, why do you not practise your new duet

with Sara? She will play nothing but valses all
the evening unless you prevent it.'

But Jill shook her head sulkily; she felt
safer in her corner. Sara was strumming on
the grand pianoforte as we passed her; her
slim fingers were running lazily over the keys,
in the 'Verliebt und Verloren' valse. Clarence
was lighting the candles: William was bringing in the coffee; and Colonel Ferguson was following rather unceremoniously. People were
always dropping in at Hyde Park Gate—perhaps Sara's bright eyes magnetised them. We
had colonels, and majors, and captains at our
will, for there was a martial craze in the house;
to-night it was grave, handsome Colonel Ferguson.

He was rather a favourite with Uncle Brian
and Aunt Philippa, perhaps because his troubles
interested them; he had buried his young wife
and child in an Indian grave, and some people
said that he had come to England to look out
for a second wife.

He was a very handsome man, and still
young enough to find favour in a girl's sight,
and his wealth made him a *grand parti* in the
parents' eyes. At present he had bestowed

equal attention on Sara and Lesbia, though close observers might have noticed that he lingered longest by Sara's side.

'How do you do, Colonel Ferguson?' said Sara, nodding to him in her bright, unconcerned way, as she finished her valse. 'Mother is over there talking to Fräulein; you will find your coffee ready for you,' and her glossy little head bent over the keys again, while the lazy music trickled through her fingers: though Colonel Ferguson did as he was told, I fancied he would keep a close watch over the young performer.

The inner drawing-room had heavy velvet hangings that closed over the archway; on cold evenings the curtains would be drawn rather closely; there would be a bright fire, and a single lamp lighted. Very often Uncle Brian would retire with his book or paper when Sara's valses wearied him or the room filled with young officers. Since Ralph's death he had certainly become rather taciturn and unsociable. Aunt Philippa, who loved gaiety, never accompanied him, but now and then Jill would creep from her corner, when her mother was not looking, and slip behind the ruby curtains. I have caught her there sometimes sitting on the rug, with her rough head against her father's knee; they would both of them look a little shamefaced, as if they were guilty of some fault.

'Go to bed, Jill; it is time for little girls to be asleep,' he would say, patting her cheek. Jill would nestle it on his coat-sleeve for a moment, as she obeyed him. Her father had the softest place in her heart. She always would have it that her mother was hard on her, but she never complained of want of kindness from her father.

'Colonel Ferguson comes very often,' remarked Lesbia, a little peevishly, as she walked to the fireplace to warm herself—she was a chilly being, and loved warmth. 'His name is Donald, is it not? some one told me so. Donald Ferguson; well, he is not bad, he may do for Sara. She has plenty of quicksilver to balance his gravity.'

I was rather surprised at this beginning; but without waiting for any answer, she went on—

'What is this Mr. Cunliffe tells me,' she asked, fixing her blue eyes on my face with

marked interest; 'you are going to carry out
your old scheme, Ursula, about nursing poor
people and singing to them. He tells me you
have chosen Heathfield for your future home,
and that he is to find you lodgings; sit down,
dear, and tell me all about it,' she went on
eagerly. 'I thought you had given up all
that when—when——' but here she stopped
and her lips trembled; of course she meant
when Charlie died, but she rarely spoke his
name. I would not let her see my astonishment—she had never seemed so sisterly before;
but I took the seat close to her and talked to
her as openly as though she were Jill or Uncle
Max; now and then I paused, and we could
hear Colonel Ferguson's deep voice—he was
evidently turning over the pages of Sara's music.

'Go on, Ursula, I like to hear it,' Lesbia
would say when I hesitated; she was not looking at me, but at the fire, with her cheek
supported against her hand.

'What do you think of it?' I asked presently, when I had finished and we had both
been silent a few minutes listening to one of
Mendelssohn's songs without words that Sara
was playing very nicely.

'What do I think of it?' she replied, and her voice startled me—it was so full of pain. 'Oh, Ursula, I think you are to be envied; if I could only come with you and work too— but there is mother, she could not do without me, and so we must just go on in the same old way.'

I was so shocked at the hopelessness of her tone, so taken aback at her words, that I could not answer her for a moment; it seemed inconceivable to me that she could be saying such things. Poor pretty Lesbia, whom Charlie had loved and whom I considered a mere fragile butterfly. She was quite pale now, and her eyes filled suddenly with tears.

'You do not believe me, Ursula; no, I was right—you never understood me. I often told dear Charlie so: you think because I laugh and dance and do as other girls do, that I have forgotten—that I do not suffer.' Do you think I shall ever find any one so good and kind in this world again?—oh! you are hard on me, and I am so miserable, so unhappy without Charlie—and I am not like you. I cannot work myself into forgetful-ness; I must stop with mother and do as she bids me, and she says it is my duty to be gay.'

I was so ashamed of myself, of my mean injustice, that I was very nearly crying myself as I asked her pardon.

'Why do you say that?' she returned almost pettishly, only she looked so miserable. 'I have nothing to forgive. I only want you to be good to me and not think the worst, for I'm really fond of you, Ursula, only you are so reserved and cold with me.'

'My poor dear,' I returned, taking the pretty face between my hands and kissing it, 'I will never be unkind to you again ; forgive me if I have misunderstood you ; for Charlie's sake I want to love you,' and then she put her head down on my shoulder and cried a little, and bemoaned herself for being so unhappy ; and all the time I comforted her my guilty conscience owned that Uncle Max was right.

CHAPTER IV.

UNCLE MAX was one of those men who like to take their own way about things ; he never hurried himself, or allowed other people's impatience to get the better of him ; 'there is a time for everything, as Solomon says,' was his favourite speech when any one reproached him with procrastination ; 'depend upon it, the best work is done slowly. What is the use of so much hurry ? when death comes we shall be sure to leave something unfinished.'

So for two whole days he just chatted commonplaces with Aunt Philippa, rallied Sara, who loved a joke, and talked politics with Uncle Brian, and never mentioned one

word about my scheme ; if I looked anxiously
at him he pretended to misunderstand my
meaning, and, in fact, behaved from morning
to night in a most provoking way.

At last I could bear it no longer, and one
wet afternoon, when I knew he was in the
drawing-room, making believe to write his
letters, but in reality getting a deal of amusement out of Sara's sprightly conversation,
for she was never silent for two minutes if she
could help it, I shut myself up in my own
room, and would not go near him. I knew
he would ask where Ursula was every half
hour, and would soon guess that I was out of
humour about something ; and possibly, in
an hour or two, his conscience would prick
him, and he would feel that I deserved re-
paration.

This little piece of ill-tempered artifice bore
excellent fruit, for before I had nearly finished
the piece of plain sewing I had set myself as a
sort of penance, there was a tap at the door,
and Sara came in, looking very excited, with
her bright eyes full of wonder.

'Oh, Ursula, there is such a fuss downstairs ! Uncle Max has been telling us all

about your absurd scheme. Mother is as cross as possible ; she is so angry, and yet half crying at the same time.'

'And Uncle Brian,' I exclaimed eagerly, ' what does he say ? '

' Oh, you know father's way. He just smiled as though the whole thing were beneath his notice, and went on reading his paper, and when mother appealed to him he said, coolly, that it was none of his business or hers either if Ursula chose to make a fool of herself; she had the right to do so—something like that, you know.'

' How very pleasant,' I remarked satirically, for I hated the way Uncle Brian put down his foot on things that displeased him. I preferred Aunt Philippa's voluble arguments to that.

' To make things worse,' went on Sara, cheerfully, ' Mrs. Fullerton and Lesbia have come in, and mother and Mrs. Fullerton are trying which can talk the faster. Lesbia asked for you, and then did not speak another word. What shall you do, Ursula, dear ? '

' I shall just go down and ask Aunt Philippa for a cup of tea,' I returned coolly, folding up my work. Sara looked half frightened at my boldness, and then she began to laugh.

'It is so absurd, you know,' she returned, linking her arm in mine affectionately. 'Whatever put such nonsense in your head; you are so comfortable here with us, and you have your own way, and I never tease you now about going to balls ; it is so silly of you trying to make yourself miserable, and living in poky lodgings. You might as well be a fakir, or a dervish, or a Protestant nun, or anything else that is unpleasant.'

'My dear, you do not know anything about it,' I answered, rather angrily. 'You and I are different people, Sara ; we shall never think the same about anything.'

'Well, I don't know,' she returned, half affronted, 'when people try to be extra good I always find they succeed in making themselves extra disagreeable. It is far more religious, in my opinion, to be pleasant to every one, and make them believe that there is something cheerful in life, instead of pulling a long face and doing such dreadfully bad things.' And after this little fling, in which she tried to be very severe, only as usual her dimples betrayed her, she begged me quite earnestly to smooth my hair, as though I were breaking one of the commandments by keeping it rough; and having obliged her in this particular, and allowed her to peep at her own pretty face over my shoulder, we went down to the drawing-room as though we were the best of friends.

It was impossible to quarrel with Sara, she was as gay and irresponsible as a child; one might as well have been angry with a butterfly for brushing his gold-powdered wings across your face; the gentle flappings of Sara's speeches never raised a momentary vexation in my mind. I was often weary of her, but then we do weary of children's company sometimes; in certain moods her bright, sparkling effervescence seemed to jar upon me, but I never liked to see her sad—sadness did not become Sara; when she cried, which was as seldom as possible, and only when some one died, or she lost a pet canary, all her beauty dimmed, and she looked limp and forlorn, like a crushed butterfly, or a draggled flower.

I do not think I was quite as cool and unconcerned as I wished to appear when I marched into the drawing-room, and after greeting Mrs. Fullerton and Lesbia, asked Aunt Philippa for a cup of tea.

Quite a hubbub of voices had struck on my ear as I opened the door, and yet complete silence met me. Lesbia, indeed, whispered 'Poor Ursula' as I kissed her, but Mrs. Fullerton looked at me with grave disapproval. Aunt Philippa was sitting bolt upright behind the tea-tray, and handed me my cup, rather as Lady Macbeth did the dagger. I received it, however, as though it were my due, and glanced at Uncle Max; but he was too wise to look at me, so I said as coolly as possible, ' Why are you so silent, and yet you were talking loudly enough before Sara and I came into the room?' For there is nothing like taking the bull of a dilemma by the horns ; and I had plenty of, let us say, native impudence, only, personally, I should have given it another name ; and then, of course, I brought the storm upon me.

Sara was right. Aunt Philippa certainly talked the faster ; Mrs. Fullerton tried her best to edge in a word now and then, a very scathing word too, but there was no silencing that flow of rapid talk. I quite envied her pure

diction and the ingenious turn of her sentences;
she made so much of her own admirable fore-
sight and care of me, and so little of my merits.

'I always said something like this would
happen, Ursula. I have told your uncle often—
Brian, why don't you speak?—yes, indeed, I have
told him often that I never met any one so
strong-minded and self-willed. You need not
laugh, Sara—unless you do it to provoke me—
but I have been like a mother to Ursula. Thank
Heaven, my daughters are not of this pattern
—they do not mistake eccentricity for goodness,
or flaunt ridiculous notions in the faces of their
elders.'

This was too bad of Aunt Philippa; only
she had lost her temper, and was feeling utterly
aggrieved, and Mrs. Fullerton, who was a
meddlesome good-humoured woman, and who
had nothing of which to complain in life except
a little over-plumpness and too much money,
was agreeing with her like a good neighbour
and friend.

Uncle Max was smiling, and pulling his
beard behind his paper; but he made no attempt
to check the flow of feminine eloquence. He had
said his say like a man, and had taken my part

behind my back, and he knew women were like new wine—very sound and sweet, but they must find their vent. Aunt Philippa would be kinder ever after if we let her scold us properly, and take our scolding with a good grace.

Once or twice Uncle Brian let his eye-glasses dangle, and spoke a peevish word or two.

'Nonsense, my dear; have I not said over and over again that this is none of our business? Ursula is old enough to know her own mind; if she chooses to be eccentric we cannot hinder her. All this talk goes for nothing.'

'Ah! but, Mr. Garston, young people want guidance,' observed Mrs. Fullerton impressively, for Aunt Philippa was beginning to sob, partly from the effects of wasted eloquence, and perhaps with a little shortness of breathing; any way her anger was working itself out. 'If you were to advise Ursula as you would Sara, your influence might induce her to change her mind.'

'I cannot endorse your opinion, Mrs. Fullerton,' returned Uncle Brian, dryly. 'I am far too keen an observer of human nature to think we can talk sense to deaf ears with any benefit. Ursula, **my** child,' turning to me with a smile that might have been kinder, but perhaps he meant it to be so—'there is not a grain of sense in your scheme; in spite of Cunliffe's eloquence, it will not hold water—in fact, in a little while you will be glad to come back to us again. When you do, I think I can promise that we will not laugh at you more than once a day, and then moderately.'

Now this speech of Uncle Brian's made me very angry. No doubt he meant to be kind, and show me that if my scheme failed I might come home to them again; but I was so much in earnest that his satire and his laughing at me hurt me more than all Aunt Philippa's hard speeches. So I flushed up, and for the first time tears came into my eyes; for he had prophesied failure, and I could not bear that, and I might have said words in my sudden irritation for which I should have been sorry afterwards, only Lesbia, who had sat behind me all this time, as silent and soft-breathed as a mouse, got up quickly and took my hand and stood by me.

'I think you have all said plenty of hard

things to Ursula, and no one has been kind to her. I think she deserves praise and not all this blame; if she cannot lead the comfortable life we do, thinking how we are to get the most pleasure and enjoy ourselves, it is because she is better than we are, and thinks more about her duty. Mrs. Garston—I do not mean to be rude, I am far too fond of you all, because you have all been so good to me,' and here Lesbia's white throat swelled—' but I cannot bear to hear Ursula so blamed. Mr. Cunliffe, I know you agree with me, you said so many nice things when Ursula was out of the room.'

This little burst of eloquence surprised us all. Uncle Max said afterwards that he was quite touched by it. Lesbia was generally so quiet and undemonstrative, that her words took Aunt Philippa by storm. She might have been offended by Lesbia saying that I was better than the rest of them, a fact that my conscience most emphatically contradicted; but when Lesbia kissed her, and begged her to think better of things, she cried a little because Charlie was not there to see how pretty she could look, and then cheered up, and made

overtures that I might come and kiss her too,
which I did most willingly, and with a full
heart, remembering she was my father's sister
and had been good to me according to her
lights.

When Uncle Max saw that reconciliation
was imminent, and that by Lesbia's help I was
likely to have the best of it, my own way, and
a good deal of petting to follow—for they would
all make more of me, during the short time
I would be with them—he threw down his
paper in high good humour and joined us.

'That is what I call sensible, Mrs. Garston,'
he said, paying her a compliment at once,
as she sat flushed and fanning herself, 'and
Ursula ought to feel herself very grateful to
you for your forbearance and acquiescence in
her plan.'

I do not believe he knew any more than
myself where the forbearance had been, but
he took it all for granted.

'Nothing puts heart into a person more
than feeling sure of one's friends' sympathy.
Now we all of us, even Garston, in spite of his
disapproval, wish Ursula good success in her
scheme; some of us think better of it than others;

for my own part, I am so convinced that she will have so many difficulties and disappointments to hamper her, that I cannot bear to say a discouraging word.' And yet he had said dozens, only I was magnanimous and forgave him.

This settled the matter, for Aunt Philippa grew so sorry for me that she was almost out of breath again pitying me. 'I do not believe she can help it,' she said, in rather an audible aside to Mrs. Fullerton; 'her mother had a sort of craze about these things, and seemed to think it part of her religion to make herself uncomfortable ; and poor Herbert was quite as bad, only he was a clergyman, and it did not matter so much with him—so I suppose the poor child inherits it. This sort of thing runs in families,' went on Aunt Philippa, in an awe-struck voice, as though it were a species of insanity. 'I am only thankful that my own girls have not got these notions.'

Mrs. Fullerton found out now that it was time to go home and dress for dinner, so Lesbia came round to me and whispered that I must come and see her soon, for she wanted to talk to me, and not to Sara, who was always running in and out.

'I am very fond of Sara, and like to see
her, she amuses me so; but when I want advice
or sympathy, I feel I must come to you now,
Ursula;' and though she had never said so
much to me before, I knew she meant it;
that there was some change in her, some
want of nature or Heaven knows what feminine need, when she missed me, and wanted
me, and found some comfort in the thought
of me.

There was no time for more discussion, and
indeed we were all a little weary of it; but
after dinner Uncle Max, who seemed in excellent spirits, as though he had done something wonderful and was proud of his own
achievements, beckoned me into the inner
drawing-room under pretence of showing
me some engravings, and when we found ourselves alone, he said pleasantly, though abruptly:

'Well, Ursula! I thought you would be
glad to have an opportunity of thanking me,
for of course you feel very grateful to me for
all the trouble I have taken.'

'Oh, indeed,' I returned scornfully, for it
would never do to encourage this vain-glorious

spirit, 'I should have felt more disposed to thank you if you had not kept me for two days in suspense.'

'That is the result of doing a woman a good turn,' shaking his head mournfully, 'the moment she gets her own way, she turns upon you and rends you; fie, fie, on you, little she-bear!'

'Oh, Max! do be quiet a moment.'

'Max, indeed! Where are your manners, child; what would Garston say if he heard your flippancy?' But by the way he stroked his beard and looked at me, I saw he was not displeased. No one would have taken him for my uncle who had seen us together, for he was a young-looking man, and I was old for my age.

'I do want you to be serious a moment,' I went on plaintively. 'I am really very obliged to you for having broken the ice; after all I have not been badly submerged. I soon rose to the surface when Lesbia held out a helping hand.'

'Well, now, Ursula; do you not agree with me—was not Lesbia a darling?'

'She was very nice and sisterly,' I confessed. 'She has more in her than I ever thought. Poor little thing; I am afraid she is very unhappy, only she hides it so.'

'Just so, that shows her good sense; the world is very intolerant of a protracted grief, its victims must learn to dry their eyes quickly.'

Uncle Max was becoming philosophical; this would never do.

'Never mind about Lesbia,' I observed impatiently, 'we can talk about her in the next room; what I want to know is, how soon I may come to Heathfield,' for I knew how dilatory men can be about other people's business, and I fully expected that Uncle Max would put me off to the summer.

'You may come as soon as you like,' he returned, rather too carelessly; 'shall we say next week, or will that be too early?'

I suppressed my astonishment cleverly, but was down on him in a moment.

'I should like to have some place found for me first,' I remarked sententiously; 'you must take lodgings for me first, and then I can settle my plans.'

'Oh, that is done already,' he observed cheerfully. 'I have spoken to Mrs. Barton

about you, and she has very nice rooms vacant.
I wanted them for Tudor, until I mooted the
Vicarage plan ; it is a tidy little place, Ursula,
and I think you will be very comfortable
there.'

I felt that Uncle Max deserved praise, and
I gave it to him without stint or limit ; he took
it nobly, like a man who feels he has earned
his reward.

' I fancy I have done a neat thing,' he said
modestly. ' Directly I read your letter and saw
that you were in earnest, I went down to Mrs.
Barton, and had a long talk with her. Do
you remember the White Cottage, Ursula, that
stands just where the road dips a little, after
you have passed the Vicarage? It is on the main
road that leads to the common—there is a field,
and one or two houses, and on the right the
road branches off to Main Street, where my
poorer parishioners live. Oh, I see you have
forgotten. Well, there is a low white cottage,
standing far back from the road, with rather
a pretty garden, and a field at the back—
people call it the White Cottage, though it is
smothered in jasmine in the summer ; and there
is a nice little parlour with a bed-room over it.

That will do capitally, I fancy. Old Mrs. Mere--
dith lived there until her death, and she left
her furniture to Mrs. Barton.'

I expressed myself as being well pleased
at this description, and then inquired a little
anxiously if there were room for my piano and
my books.

'Oh yes, it is quite a good-sized room ; that
is why I wanted it for Tudor ; you will not
mind it being a little low—it is only a cottage,
remember. There is a nice easy couch, I spotted
that at once, and a capital easy-chair, and
some corner cupboards that will hold a store
of good things ; you can make it as pretty as
possible.'

'And Mrs. Barton, Max; is she a pleasant
person ? '

'There could not be a pleasanter. You will
find yourself in clover, Ursula, you will indeed ;
she is a nice little woman, and has all the car-
dinal virtues, I believe ; she is a widow, and has
a big son who works at Roberts's, the builders.
Nathaniel is very big, very big indeed, so much
so that I feel it my duty to warn you of his size,
for fear you should receive a shock. The cottage
just holds him when he sits down, and his

mother's one anxiety is that he should not bring
down the kitchen ceiling more than once a year,
as it hurts his head and comes expensive ; he
has a black collie they call Tinker, the cleverest
dog in the place so Nathaniel says—and these
three constitute the household of the White
Cottage.'

I was charmed with Uncle Max's account ;
the cottage seemed cosy and homelike. I knew
I could trust his opinion ; he was a good judge
of character, and was seldom wrong in his
estimate of a man, woman, or child, and he
would be especially careful to entrust me to a
thoroughly reliable person. I begged him therefore to close with Mrs. Barton at once ; she
asked a very moderate price for her rooms, and
I could have afforded higher terms.   It would
not take me long to pack my books and other
treasures—some of them I should be obliged to
leave behind ; but I must take all Charlie's books
and my own, and my favourite pictures and bits
of china, and a store of fine linen for my own
use. I was somewhat demoralised by the luxury
at Hyde Park Gate, and liked to make myself
comfortable after my own way. Poor Charlie
used to laugh at me and say I should be an old

maid, and as I considered this fact inevitable, I took his teasing in good part.

I told Uncle Max that I thought I could be ready in another week, and that I saw no good in delay. He assented to this, and was kind enough to add that the sooner I came the better. I was a little dismayed to find that he had not considered himself bound to keep my counsel ; he had talked about my plan to his curate, Mr. Tudor, and I gathered from his manner, for he refused to tell me any more, that he had discussed it with another person.

This was too bad, but I would not let him see that this vexed me. I wanted to settle in and begin my work quietly before the neighbourhood knew of my existence, but if Uncle Max published my intended arrival in every house he visited, I felt I could not even worship in comfort for fear the congregation should be eyeing me suspiciously.

I thought it better to change the subject, so I began to question him about Mr. Tudor and Mrs. Drabble, the latter being the ruling power at the Vicarage ; and he fell upon the bait and swallowed it eagerly, so my vexation passed unnoticed.

Uncle Max did not live quite alone. His house was large, far too large for an unmarried man, and he was very sociable by nature, so he induced his curate to take up his abode with him; but the two men and Mrs. Drabble, the housekeeper, and the maid under her could not fill it, and several rooms were shut up. Lawrence Tudor had been a pupil of Uncle Max, and the two were very much attached to each other. Uncle Max had brought him up once or twice to Hyde Park Gate, and we had all been much pleased with him. He was not in the least good-looking, but I remember Sara said he was gentlemanly, and pleasant, and had a nice voice. I knew his frank manner and evident affection for Uncle Max prepossessed me in his favour; he had been very athletic in his college days, and was passionately fond of boating and cricket, and he was very musical and sang splendidly.

The little Uncle Max had told me about him had strongly interested me. The Tudors had been wealthy people, and Uncle Max had spent more than one long vacation at their house, coaching Walter Tudor, who was going in for an army examination, and reading Greek with

Lawrence, or Laurie, as they generally called him, and another brother, Ben.

Lawrence had meant to enter the army too. Nelson, the eldest of all, was already in India, and had a captaincy. They were all fine, stalwart young men, fond of riding and hunting, and any out-of-door pursuit. But there never would have been a parson among them but for the failure of the company in which Mr. Tudor's money was invested. He had been one of the directors, and from wealth he was reduced to poverty.

There was no money to buy Walter a commission, so he enlisted, bringing fresh trouble to his parents by doing so. Ben entered an office, but Lawrence was kept at Oxford, by an uncle's generosity, and under strong pressure consented to take Orders.

The poor young fellow had no special vocation, and he owned to Max afterwards that he feared that he had done the wrong thing. I am afraid Max thought so too, but he would not discourage him by saying so ; on the contrary he treated him in a bracing manner, telling him that he had put his hand to the plough and that there must be no looking backward,

and bidding him pluck up heart and do his
duty as well as he could; and then he smoothed
his way by asking him to be his curate and
live with him, so saving him from the loneli-
ness and discomfort of some curates' existence,
who are at the mercy of their landladies and
laundresses.

So the two lived merrily together, and
Lawrence Tudor was all the better man and
parson for Uncle Max's genial help and sympathy; and though Mrs. Drabble grumbled and
did not take kindly to him at first, she made
him thoroughly comfortable, and mended his
socks and sewed on his buttons in motherly
fashion. Mrs. Drabble was quite a character
in her way; she was a fair, fussy little woman,
who looked meek enough to warrant the best
of tempers; she had a soft voice and manner
that deceived you, and a vague rambling sort
of talk that landed you nowhere; but if ever
woman could be a mild virago Mrs. Drabble
was that woman. She worshipped her master,
and never allowed any one to find fault with
him; but with Mr. Tudor, or the maid, or any
one who interfered with her, she could be a
flaxen-haired termagant—she could scold in a

low voice for half an hour together without minding a single stop or pausing to take breath. Mr. Tudor used to laugh at her, or get out of her way, when he had had enough of it; she only tried it on her master once, but Max stood and stared at her with such surprise and such puzzled good humour that she grew ashamed and stopped in the very middle of a sentence.

But with all her temper neither of them could have spared Mrs. Drabble, she made them so comfortable.

CHAPTER V.

'WHEN THE CAT IS AWAY.'

AUNT PHILIPPA had one very good point in her character : she was not of a nagging disposition. When she scolded she did it thoroughly, and was perhaps a long time doing it, but she never carried it into the next day.

Jill always said her mother was too indolent for a prolonged effort, but then poor Jill often said naughty things—but we all of us knew that Aunt Philippa's wrath soon evaporated; it made her hot and uncomfortable while it lasted, and she was glad to be quit of it, so she refrained herself prudently when I spoke of my approaching departure; and being of a bustling temperament, and not averse to changes unless they gave her much trouble, she took a great deal of interest in my arrangements, and bought a nice little travelling-clock that she said would be useful to me.

Seeing her so pleasant and reasonable, I made a humble petition that Jill might be set free from some of her lessons to help me pack my books and ornaments. She made a little demur at this and offered Draper's services instead; but it was Jill I wanted, for the poor child was fretting sadly about my going away, and I thought it would comfort her to help me. So after a time Aunt Philippa relented, after extorting a promise from Jill that she would work all the harder after I had gone; and as young people seldom think about the future except in the way of foolish dreams, Jill cheerfully gave her word. So for the last few days we were constantly together, and Fräulein had an unexpected holiday. Jill worked like a horse in my service, and only broke one Dresden group; she came to me half crying with the fragment in her hand—the poor little shepherdess had lost her head as well as her crook, and the pink coat of the shepherd had an unseemly rent in it; but I only laughed at the disaster, and would not scold her for her

awkwardness. China had a knack of slipping
through Jill's fingers, she had a loose uncertain
grasp of things that were brittle and delicate,
she had not learnt to control her muscles or
restrain her strength. She had a way of lifting
me up when I teased her that turns me giddy
to remember; I was quite a child in her hands.
She was always ashamed of herself when
she had done it, and begged my pardon, and
as long as she put me on my feet again I was
ready to forgive anything. Jill felt a sort of
forlorn consolation in using up her strength in
my service, she would hardly let me do anything myself; I might sit down and order her
about from morning to night if I chose.

I made her very happy by leaving some of
my possessions under her care—some books
that I knew she would like to read, and other
treasures that I had locked up in my wardrobe.
Jill had the key and could rummage if she
liked, but she told me quite seriously that it
would comfort her to come and look at them
sometimes—'It will feel as though you were
coming back some day, Ursie,' she said affectionately.

Late one afternoon I left her busy in my

room, and went to the Albert Hall Mansions to
bid good-bye to Lesbia. I had called once or
twice, but had always missed her. So I slipped
across in the twilight, as I thought at that
hour they would have returned from their
drive.

The Albert Hall Mansions were only a
stone's throw from Uncle Brian's house, so I considered myself safe from any remonstrance on
Aunt Philippa's part. I liked to go there in the
soft, early dusk; the smooth noiseless ascent of
the lift, and the lighted floors that we passed,
gave one an odd, dreamy feeling. Mrs. Fullerton
had a handsome suite of apartments on the
third floor, and there was a beautiful view from
her drawing-room window of the Park and the
Albert Memorial. It was a nice, cheerful
situation, and Mrs. Fullerton, who liked gaiety,
preferred it to Rutherford Lodge, though
Lesbia had been born there, and she had passed
her happiest days in it.

I found Mrs. Fullerton alone, but she
seemed very friendly, and was evidently glad
to see me. I suppose I was better company
than her own thoughts.

I liked Mrs. Fullerton, after a temperate

fashion. She was a nice little woman, and would have been nicer still if she had talked less and thought more. But when one's words lie at the tip of one's tongue there is little time for reflection, and there is sure to be tares amongst the wheat.

She was looking serious this evening, but that did not interfere with her comeliness, or her pleasant manners. I found her warmth gratifying, and prepared to unbend more than usual.

'Sit down, my dear. No, not on that chair, take the easy one by the fire. You are looking rather fagged, Ursula. It seems to be the fashion with young people now they get middle-aged before their time. Oh yes, Lesbia is out. It is the Engleharts' " At Home," and she promised to go with Mrs. Pierrepoint. But she will be back soon. Now we are alone, I want to ask you a question. I am rather anxious about Lesbia. Dr. Spratt says there is a want of tone about her. She is too thin, and her appetite is not good. The child gets prettier every day, but she looks far too delicate.'

I could not deny this. Lesbia certainly looked far from strong, and then she took cold

so easily. I hinted that perhaps late hours and
so much visiting (for the Fullertons had an
immense circle of acquaintances, with possibly
half a dozen friends amongst them) might be
bad for her.

Mrs. Fullerton looked rather mournful at
this.

'I hope you have not put that in her head,'
she returned uneasily. 'All yesterday she
was begging me to give up the place and go
back to Rutherford Lodge. Major Parkhurst is
going to India in February, and so the house
will be on our hands.'

'I think the change will be good for Lesbia.
It is such a pretty place, and she was always so
fond of it.'

'Oh, it is pretty enough,' with a discontented
air; 'but life in a village is a very tame affair.
There are not more than four families in the
whole place whom we can visit, and when we
want a little gaiety we have to drive into
Pinkerton.'

'I think it would be good for Lesbia's
health, Mrs. Fullerton.'

'Well, well,' a little peevishly, 'we must
talk to Dr. Pratt about it. But how is Lesbia

to settle well if I bury her in that poky little
village? Perhaps I ought not to say so to you,
Ursula; but poor dear Charlie has been dead
these two years, so there can be no harm in
speaking of such things now. But Sir Henry
Sinclair is here a great deal, and there is no
mistaking his intentions, only Lesbia keeps him
at such a distance.'

I thought it very bad taste of Mrs. Fullerton
always to talk to me about Lesbia's suitors.
Lesbia never mentioned such things herself.
As far as I could judge, she was very shy
with them all. I could not believe that the
placid young baronet had any chance with
her. She might possibly marry, but poor
Charlie's successor would hardly be a thick-
set, clumsy young man, with few original ideas
of his own. Colonel Ferguson would have
been far better, but he evidently preferred
Sara.

I was spared any reply, for Lesbia entered
the room at that moment. She looked more
delicately fair than usual, perhaps because of
the contrast with her heavy furs. Her hair
shone like gold under her little velvet bonnet,
but though she was so warmly dressed she

shivered and crept as close as possible to the fire.

Mrs. Fullerton had some notes to write, so she went into the dining-room to write them, and very good-naturedly left us by ourselves.

Lesbia looked at me rather wistfully.

'I have missed you twice, Ursula. I am so sorry; and now you go the day after to-morrow. I wish I could do something for you. Is there nothing you could leave in my charge?'

'Only Jill,' I said, half laughing. 'If you would take a little more notice of her after I have gone, I should be so thankful to you.'

I thought Lesbia seemed somewhat amused at the request.

'Poor old Jill. I will do my best, but she never will talk to me. I think I should like her better than Sara, if she would only open her lips to me. Well, Ursula, what have you and mother been talking about?'

'About Rutherford Lodge,' I returned quickly. 'Do you really want to go back there?'

'Did mother talk about that?' looking

excessively pleased. 'Oh yes, I am longing to
go back. I don't want to frighten you, Ursie,
dear—and, indeed, there is no need—but this
life is half killing me. I am too close to Hyde
Park Gate—one never gets a chance of for-
getting old troubles; and then mother is always
saying gaiety is good for me, and she will
accept every invitation that comes—and I get
so horribly tired; and then one cannot fight so
well against depression.'

I took her hand silently, but made no
answer; but I suppose she felt my sympathy.

'You must not think I am wicked and
rebellious,' she went on with a sigh. 'I promised dear Charlie to be brave, and not let
the trouble spoil my life; he would have it
that I was so young that happiness must return
after a time, and so I mean to do my best to be
happy, for mother's sake, as well as my own;
and I know Charlie would not like me to go on
grieving,' with a sad little smile.

'No, darling, and I quite understand you.'
And she cheered up at that.

'I knew you would, and that is why I want
to tell you things. I have tried to do as
mother wished, but I do not think her plan

answers; excitement carries one away, and one can be as merry as other girls for a time, but it all comes back worse than ever.'

'Mere gaiety never satisfied an aching heart yet.'

'No; I told mother so, and I begged her to go back to Rutherford because it is so quiet and peaceful there, and I think I shall be happier. I shall have my garden and conservatory, and there will be plenty of riding and tennis. I am very fond of our vicar's wife, Mrs. Trevor, and I rather enjoy helping her in the Sunday School and at the mothers' meeting; not that I do much, for I am not like you, Ursula, but I like to pretend to be useful sometimes.'

'I see what you mean, Lesbia; your life will be more natural and less strained than it is here.'

'Yes, and time will hang less heavy on my hands. I do love gardening, Ursula. I know I shall forget my troubles when I find myself with dear old Patrick again, grumbling because I will pick the roses. I shall sleep better in my little room, and wake less unhappy. Oh, mother!' as Mrs. Fullerton entered at that moment with a half finished note in her hand, 'I am telling Ursula how home-sick I am, and how I long for the dear old Lodge. Do let us go back, mother darling, I want to hunt for violets again in the little shady hollow beyond the lime-tree walk.'

'Yes, dearest, we will go if you really wish it so much,' returned Mrs. Fullerton, with a sigh. 'Why, my pet, did you think I should refuse?' as Lesbia put her arms round her neck, and thanked her. 'When a mother has only got one child she is not likely to deny her much, is she, Ursula?'

'Oh, mother, how good you are to me!' returned Lesbia, and her blue eyes were shining with joy. When Mrs. Fullerton had left the room again she told me that she had often cried herself to sleep with the longing to be in her old home again; she loved every flower in the garden, every animal about the place, and she grew quite bright and cheerful as she planned out her days. No, there was nothing morbid about Lesbia's nature; she was an honest, well-meaning girl, who had had a great disappointment in her life; she meant to outlive it if she could, to be as happy as possible. A wise in-

stinct told her that her best chance of healing
lay in country sights and sounds—the fresh
gallop over the downs, the pleasant saunter
through the sweet Sussex lanes, the sweet
breath of her roses and carnations would all
woo her back to health and cheerfulness.
When the pretty colour came back into Lesbia's
face her mother would not regret her sacrifice ;
and then I remembered that Charlie's friend,
Harcourt Manners, lived about half a dozen
miles from Rutherford, and always attended the
Pinkerton dances, and he was a nice intelligent fellow. But I scolded back the foolish
thoughts, and felt ashamed of myself for entertaining them.

I parted from Lesbia very affectionately, for
she seemed loth to say good-bye, but I knew
poor Jill would be grumbling at my absence—
the others were dining out, and I had promised
to join the schoolroom tea, which was to be
half an hour later on my account, but it was
nearly six before I made my appearance—very
penitent at my delay, and fully expecting a
scolding.

I found Jill, however, kneeling on the rug
making toast, with Sooty in her arms ; she had

blacked her face in her efforts, but looked in high good humour.

'Fräulein has gone out for the whole evening —that freckled Fräulein Misschenstock has been here, and has invited her to tea and supper. Mamma said she could go, as you would remain with me, so we shall be alone and cosy for the whole evening. Now, you may pour out tea, if you like, for I have all this buttered toast on my mind. I am as hungry as a hunter; but there is a whole seed-cake I am glad to see. Now, darling, be quick, for you have kept me so long waiting,' and Jill brushed vigorously at her blackened cheek, and beamed at me.

But, alas! we had reckoned without our host, and a grand disappointment was in store for us, though, as it turned out, things were not as bad as they appeared to be at first.

I was praising Jill's buttered toast, for I knew she prided herself on this delicacy, and she had just cut herself a thick wedge of the seed-cake, which she was discussing with a schoolgirl's appetite, when I heard Uncle Brian's voice calling for Ursula rather loudly, so I ran to the head of the staircase, and to my surprise saw him coming up in his slow dignified manner.

'Look here, Ursula, I shall be late at the Pollocks', and your aunt and Sara have gone on, and there is Tudor in the drawing-room, just arrived with a message from Cunliffe. Of course we must put him up; but the trouble is there is no dinner, and, of course, he is famished—young men always are.'

My heart sank as I thought of Jill, but there was no help for it. Max's friends were sacred. Mr. Tudor must be made as comfortable as possible.

'It cannot be helped, Uncle Brian,' I returned, trying to keep the vexation I felt out of my voice, 'supposing you send Mr. Tudor up to the schoolroom, and we will give him some tea. Jill has made some excellent buttered toast, and Clayton can get some supper for him by-and-by in the dining-room, there is sure to be a cold joint—or perhaps Mrs. Martin will have something cooked for him.

'That must do,' he replied, somewhat relieved at this advice; 'we shall be back soon after tea, so you will not have him long on your hands; entertain him as well as you can, there's a good girl.' He had quite forgotten, and so had I for the moment, that Fräulein was out for the evening, and that possibly Aunt Philippa might object to a young man joining the schoolroom tea ; but as it proved afterwards, she was more shocked at Uncle Brian than at any one else—she said he ought to have given up his dinner and stayed with his guest.

'I confess I do not see what Ursula could have done better,' she remarked severely ; ' she could not spend the evening alone with him in the drawing-room—and of course he wanted his tea ; that comes of allowing Fräulein to neglect her duties, she is too fond of spending her time with Fräulein Misschenstock.'

I did not dare break the news to Jill, for fear she should lock herself in her own room, for she never liked the society of young men— they laughed at her too much, in a civil sort of way ; so I hurried down into the drawing-room and explained matters to Mr. Tudor, whom I found walking about the room and looking somewhat ill at ease.

He seemed rather amused at the idea of the schoolroom tea, but owned that he was hungry and tired, as he had had a fourteen-mile walk that day.

'It is all Mr. Cunliffe's fault that I am quartered on you in this way,' he said, laughing a little nervously—and very likely Uncle Brian's dignified reception had made him uncomfortable ; 'but he would insist on my bringing my bag, and Mr. Garston has a dinner engagement, and cannot attend to business until to-morrow morning.'

'I am afraid you would like a dinner engagement, too, after your fourteen miles,' I returned, in a sympathetic voice, for he did look very tired. 'We will give you some tea now, and then you can get rid of the dust of the journey, and by that time Mrs. Martin will have done her best to provide you with some supper.'

'I see I have fallen in good hands,' he replied, brightening at this in a boyish sort of way. 'Where is the schoolroom? I did not know there was such an apartment, but of course Mrs. Garston told me that her youngest daughter had not finished her studies. I think I saw her once—she was very tall, and had dark hair.'

'Oh yes, that was Jill—I mean Jocelyn, but we always call her Jill. Will you come this way, please. Fräulein is out, and we were having a good time by ourselves.'

'And I have come to spoil it,' he answered regretfully, as I opened the door. I shall never forget Jill's face when she saw us on the threshold. She quite forgot to shake hands with Mr. Tudor in her dismay, but stood hunching her shoulders, with Sooty still clasped in her arms and her great eyes staring at him, till he said a pleasant word to her, and then she flushed up, and subsided into her chair. I stole an anxious glance at the cake; to my great relief Jill had been quietly proceeding with her meal in my absence, for I knew that in her chagrin she would refuse to touch another morsel. I wondered a little what Mr. Tudor would think of her ungracious reception of him; but he showed his good breeding by taking no notice of it, and confining his remarks to me.

Jill's ill-humour thawed by-and-by when she saw how he entered into the spirit of the fun. He vaunted his own skill with the toasting-fork, and in spite of fatigue insisted on super-

intending another batch of the buttered toast ;
he was very particular about the clearness of
the fire, and delivered quite an harangue on
the subject. Jill's sulky countenance relaxed
by-and-by, she opened her lips to contradict
him, and was met so skilfully that she appealed
to me for assistance.

By the time tea was over, we were as
friendly with Mr. Tudor as though we had
known him all our lives, and Jill was laughing
heartily over his racy descriptions of schoolroom feasts and other escapades of his youth.
He looked absurdly young in spite of his
clerical dress, he had a bright face and a pecu-
liarly frank manner that made me trust him at
once ; he did not look particularly clever, and
Jill had the best of him in argument, but one
felt instinctively that he was a man who would
never do a mean or unkind action, that he
would tell the truth to his own detriment with
a simple honesty that made up for lack of
talent.

I could see that Jill's bigness and clever-
ness surprised him. He evidently found her
amusing, for he tried to draw her out ; perhaps he liked to see how her great eyes opened

and then grew bright, as she tossed back her black locks or shook them impatiently. When Jill was happy and at ease her face would grow illuminated; her varying expression, her animation, her quaint picturesque talk, made her thoroughly interesting. I was never dull in Jill's company, she had always something fresh to say, she had a fund of originality, and drew her words newly coined from her own mint.

I do not believe that Mr. Tudor quite understood her, for he was a simple young fellow. But she piqued his curiosity. I must have appeared quite a tame, commonplace person beside her. When Jill went out of the room to fetch something, he asked me, rather curiously, how old she was, and when I told him that she was a mere child, not quite sixteen, he said, half musing, 'that she seemed older than that. She knew so much about things, but he supposed she was very clever.'

We went down into the drawing-room after this, and Jill kept me company while Mr. Tudor supped in state, with Clayton and Clarence to wait on him. He came up after a very short interval, and said, half laughing, ' that his supper had been a most formal affair.'

' By the bye, Miss Garston,' he observed, as though by an afterthought, ' I hear you are coming down to Heathfield.' He stole a glance at Jill as he spoke. She had discarded her Indian muslin and coral necklace as being too grand for the occasion, and wore her ruby velveteen that always suited her admirably. She looked very nice, and quite at her ease, sitting half buried in Uncle Brian's armchair, instead of being bolt upright in her corner. She had drawn her big feet carefully under her gown, and was quite a presentable young lady.

I thought Mr. Tudor was rather impressed with the transformation—Cinderella in her brown schoolroom frock, with a smutty cheek and rumpled collar, was quite a different person —presto—change—the young princess in the ruby dress has smooth locks and a thick gold necklace. She has big shining eyes and a happy child's laugh. Her little white teeth gleam in the lamplight. I do not wonder in the least that Mr. Tudor looks at Jill as he talks to me. It is a habit people have with me.

But I answered him quite graciously.

'Yes, I am coming down to Heathfield the day after to-morrow. I suppose I ought to say *Deo volente.* I hope you all mean to be good to me, Mr. Tudor, and not laugh at my poor little pretensions.'

'I shall not laugh, for one,' he replied, looking me full in the face now with his honest eyes. 'I think it is a good work, Miss Garston. The Vicar'—he always called Uncle Max the Vicar—'was talking about it up at Gladwyn the other day, and Mr. Hamilton said——'

'Gladwyn? Is that the name of a house?' I asked, interrupting Mr. Tudor a little abruptly.

'To be sure. Have you not heard of Gladwyn?' And at that he looked a little amused; but I was not fated to hear more of Gladwyn that night, for the next moment Aunt Philippa came bustling into the room, and Sara and Uncle Brian followed her.

CHAPTER VI.

THE WHITE COTTAGE.

GOOD-BYE is an unpleasant word to say, and I said mine as quickly as possible, but I did not like the remembrance of Jill's wet cheek that I had kissed—I was haunted by it during the greater part of my brief journey. For some inexplicable reason I had chosen to arrive at Heathfield late in the afternoon ; I wanted to slip into my new home in the dusk. I knew that Uncle Max would meet me at the station, and look after my luggage, so I should have no trouble, and I hoped that I should wake up among my neighbours the next morning before they knew of my arrival.

When we stopped at some station a little while before we reached Heathfield, the guard put a gentleman in my compartment—I fancied

they had not noticed me, for a large black
retriever followed him.

The gentleman lifted his hat directly he
saw me, and apologised for his dog's presence,
until I assured him it made no difference to me ;
and then he drew a newspaper from his bag
and tried to read by the somewhat flickering
light. As I had nothing else to do, and his
attention was evidently very much absorbed, I
looked at him from time to time in an idle,
furtive sort of way.

He had taken off his hat and put it on the
seat ; his dark smooth shaven face reminded me
of a Romish priest, but he had no tonsure ;
instead of that he had thick closely cropped
hair without a hint or suspicion of baldness,
was strongly built and very broad, and looked
like a man who had undergone training.

I was rather given to study the countenance of my fellow passengers—it was a way I
had—but I was not particularly prepossessed
with this man's face ; it looked hard and stern,
and his manner, though perfectly gentlemanly,
was a little brusque. I abandoned the Romish
priest theory after a second glance, and told
myself he was more like a Roman gladiator.

As we approached Heathfield, he folded up
his paper and patted his dog, who had sat all
this time at his feet, with his head on his knees.
It was a beautiful, intelligent animal, and
had soft eyes like a woman, and by the way
he wagged his tail and licked the hand that
fondled his glossy head, I saw he was devoted
to his master.

Just then I encountered a swift, searching
glance from the stranger, which rather surprised
me. He had looked at me as he spoke in an
indifferent way; but this second look was a
little perplexing; it was as though he had
suddenly recognised me, and that the fact
amused him, and yet we had never met before,
—it was such an uncommon face, so singular
altogether, that I could never have forgotten it.

I grew irritated without reason, for how
could a stranger recognise me? Happily the
lights from the station flashed before my eyes
at that moment, and I began nodding and
smiling towards a corner by the bookstall,
where a felt hat and brown head were all that
I could see of Uncle Max.

' Well, here you are, Ursula, punctual to a
minute,' exclaimed Max, as he shook hands.

' Halloa, Hamilton, where did you spring from?'
going to the carriage door to speak to my
fellow-passenger. I was so provoked at this,
fearing an introduction, for Max was such a
friendly soul, that I went to the luggage-van,
and began counting my boxes, and Max did
not hurry himself to look after me.

' Now then,' he observed cheerily, when he
condescended to join me, ' is your luggage all
right? Do you mean all those traps are yours;
bless me, Ursula, what will Mrs. Barton say?
Put them on the fly, you fellows, and be sharp
about it. Come along, child, it is pelting cats
and dogs, if you know what that means; you
have a wet welcome to Heathfield.'

I took the news philosophically, and assured
him it did not matter in the least. We could
hear the rain beating against the windows as
we reached the booking office. A closed waggonette with a pair of horses was waiting at the
door; my fellow passenger, whom Max had
addressed as Hamilton, was standing on the
pavement, speaking somewhat angrily to the
coachman. I heard the man's answer as he
touched his hat.

' Miss Darrell said I was to bring the waggonette, sir; it did not rain so badly when the order was brought round to the stables.'

'I could have taken a fly easily; it is worse than folly bringing out the horses this wet night. Jump in, Nap. What, must I go first? Manners before a wet coat.'

I heard no more, for Max hurried me into a fly, and the waggonette passed us on the road.

'Who was that?' I asked curiously.

'Oh, that is Mr. Hamilton. Why did you not wait for me to introduce him to you, Ursula? He is a rich doctor who lives in these parts; he practises for his own pleasure among the poor people; he will not attend gentle-folks. He told me that he had studied medicine meaning to make it his profession, but a distant relative died and left him a fortune, and by so doing spoiled his career.'

'That was rather ungracious of him; but he looks the sort of man who could do plenty of grumbling. Where does he live, Max?'

'Oh, at Gladwyn; I cannot show you the house now, because we do not pass it. There is the church, Ursula, and there is Tudor in his macintosh coming out of the Vicarage— that is the best of Lawrence, he never shirks his duty; he hates the job, but he does it. He is going down to see old Smithers, and get sworn at for his pains.'

'Have you got any cases ready for me, Max?' I asked, with a little tingling of excitement.

'Hamilton has. I was at Gladwyn the other evening, and had a talk with him. He was a little offhand about your mission; he thinks you must be romantic, and all that sort of thing. You would have laughed to have heard him talk, and I let him go on just for the joke of it. It was rich to hear him say that he did not believe in hysterical goodness; a girl would do anything now to get herself talked about—no, I did not mean to repeat that,' interrupting himself, with an annoyed air. 'Hamilton always says more than he means. Look, Ursula, there is the White Cottage; that bow window to the right belongs to your parlour. Now, my dear, I will open the gate, and you must just run up the path as quickly as you can, for you can hardly hold up an umbrella in this wind. You see the cottage does not boast of a carriage drive.'

That odious Mr. Hamilton—or Dr. Hamilton,

which was it? No wonder he looked like a
Romish priest if he could make those Jesuitical
remarks! I felt I almost hated him, but I resolved to banish him from my mind, as I ran
past the dripping laurels that bordered the
narrow path. The cottage door was open as
soon as our fly had stopped at the gate; and
by the light I could see the neat flower borders
and clipped yews, and a leafless wide-spreading
tree with a seat under it. As I made my way
into the porch, a very big man without his
coat passed me with a civil 'good evening.' I
thought it must be Nathaniel, from his great
height, and, of course, the prim-looking little
widow in black, standing on the threshold, was
Mrs. Barton. She had a nice plaintive face,
and spoke in a mild deprecating voice.

'Good evening, Mrs. Barton. What dreadful weather; I hope my wet boxes will not
spoil the oilcloth.'

'That is easily wiped off, Miss Garston; but
I am thinking the damp must have made you
chilly; come into the parlour, there is a fine
rousing fire that will soon warm you. A fire
is a deal of comfort on a wet, cool night; I
have lighted one in your bed-room, too.'

Evidently Mrs. Barton spared herself no trouble. I was a fire-worshipper, and loved to see the ruddy flame lighting up all the odd corners, and I was glad to think both my rooms would be cheerful. The parlour looked the picture of comfort ; my piano was nicely placed, and the davenport, and the chair that I had sent with it. A large old-fashioned couch was drawn across the window, the round table had a white cloth on it, and the tea-tray and a cottage loaf were suggestive of a meal. The room was long and rather low, but the bow window gave it a cosy aspect ; one glance satisfied me that I had space for the principal part of my books, the rest could be put in my bedroom. When Mrs. Barton stirred the fire and lighted the candles the room looked extremely cheerful ; especially as Tinker, the collie, had taken a fancy to the rug, and had stretched himself upon it after giving me a wag of his tail as a welcome. Mrs. Barton would hardly give me time to warm my hands before she begged me to follow her upstairs and take off my things while they brought in the luggage.

I found my bed-room had one peculiarity, you had to descend two broad steps before you entered it.

It was the same size as the parlour, and had a bow window. The furniture was unusually good; it had belonged to the previous lodger, Mrs. Meredith, who had bequeathed it to Mrs. Barton at her death.

I was thankful to see a pretty iron bedstead with a brass ring and blue chintz hangings, instead of the four-poster I had dreaded. There was a commodious cupboard and a handsome Spanish mahogany chest of drawers that Mrs. Barton pointed out with great pride. A bright fire burnt in the blue-tiled fireplace; there was an easy-chair and a round table in the bow window; a pleasant perfume of lavender-scented sheets pervaded the room, and a winter nosegay of red and white chrysanthemums was prettily arranged in a curious china bowl. I praised everything to Mrs. Barton's satisfaction, and then she went downstairs to see to the tea, first giving me the information that Nathaniel was coming upstairs with the big trunk, and would I tell him where to place it.

He entered the next moment, carrying the heavy trunk on his shoulder as easily as though it were a toy. He was a good-looking man with a fair beard and a pair of honest blue eyes, and in spite of his size and strength—for he was a perfect son of Anak—seemed rather shy and retiring.

I left him loosening the straps of my box, and went downstairs to find Uncle Max.

He had made himself quite at home, and was sitting in the big easy-chair contemplating the fire.

' Well, Ursula, how do you like your rooms? Oh yes, there are two cups and saucers,' as I looked inquiringly at the table, ' because Mrs. Barton expects me to remain to tea. She is frying ham and eggs at the present moment—I hope you do not mind such homely country fare, but to-morrow you will be your own housekeeper.'

I assured Uncle Max that I had fallen in love with the White Cottage, and that I liked Mrs. Barton excessively, that my bedroom was especially cosy and was most comfortably furnished. ' You will see how pretty this room will look when I put up my new curtains and pictures,' I went on ; ' it is a little bare at present, but it will soon have a more furnished appearance. I mean to be so busy to-morrow settling all my treasures,' and I spoke with so

much animation that Uncle Max smiled at what
he called my youthful enthusiasm.

'You may be as busy as you like all day,'
he returned in his pleasant way, 'so that you
come up to the Vicarage in the afternoon to
see Mrs. Drabble.   Lawrence will be out—that
fellow always is out'—in a humorous tone of
vexation.   'He makes himself so confoundedly
agreeable that people are always asking him to
dinner—he is terribly secular, is Lawrence, but
he is young and will mend; come up to the
Vicarage and dine with me, Ursula; I want
you to taste Mrs. Drabble's pancakes, they are
food for angels, as Lawrence always says.'

I accepted the invitation a little regretfully,
for it seemed hard to leave my hermitage the
first evening, but then Uncle Max had been
so good to me that it would never do to disappoint him, and as Mr. Tudor would be out
we should be very cosy together.

Mrs. Barton brought in the ham and eggs
at this moment, and I sat down before my
gay little tea-tray, marvelling secretly at the
scarlet flamingo.   There were plenty of homely
delicacies on the table : hot cakes and honey,
and a basket of brown and yellow pippins.

Uncle Max shook his head and pretended the hot cakes would ruin his digestion, but he enjoyed them all the same, and made an excellent meal.

We sat for a long time talking over the fire, chiefly of Lesbia and Jill, for he took a warm interest in them both ; but about eight o'clock he remembered he had an engagement, and went off rather hurriedly, and I went upstairs and unpacked one of my boxes, and arranged my clothes in the chest of drawers and in the big, roomy cupboard.

When the church-clock struck ten, I went down again in search of hot water. At the sound of my footstep, Mrs. Barton came out in the passage and invited me into the kitchen.

'There is only Nat there at his books,' she said, in her plaintive voice ; 'he works late sometimes, though I tell him he uses up candle and fire-light. Please make yourself at home, Miss Garston, we shall always be pleased to see you in our kitchen, when you like to pop in.'

'I hope I shall not come too often,' I returned, looking round at its bright snug appearance. A square of dark carpet covered part of the red-tiled floor, the round deal table in the centre was hidden under a crimson cloth, two big elbow-chairs stood on each side of the wide fireplace. Nathaniel sat in one with a little round table in front of him, covered with books and papers, with a small lamp for his own use. Mrs. Barton's workbox and mending basket were on the centre table, the hearth had just been swept up, there was a smell of hot bread, and a row of freshly baked loaves were cooling on the dresser; the firelight shone on the gleaming pewter and brass utensils, and a great tabby cat sat purring on the elbow of Nathaniel's chair. I thought he seemed a little confused at my entrance, for he got up rather awkwardly and shuffled his papers together, so I took pity on his embarrassment, and only spoke to Mrs. Barton.

She took me into the little outer kitchen to show me where she did her cooking, and I asked her in a low voice what he was studying.

'He does a little of everything,' she said, with a sort of suppressed pride in her voice. 'Sometimes it is history, and oftener summing; he will have it that a man cannot have too much learning, and that he wants to improve himself; he is always fretting because he never had a chance when he was young, all along of his having to work when his poor father died, and so he is all for making up for lost time; sometimes Dr. Hamilton comes in and helps him with the Latin and—what do you call those figures?'

I suggested mathematics—and she nodded assent.

'Oh, Nat is a sight cleverer already than his master,' she went on. 'I am thinking that if he goes on learning more and more that Mr. Roberts will be taking him into the business some day. Nat is a sort of foreman now, for his master thinks a deal of Nathaniel, and no wonder, for it is not only his learning, and his sitting up late, and getting up early in the winter's morning, and creeping downstairs without his boots so as not to wake me; for all he is such a good son; but I will say it that there is not a young man in these parts that can beat Nat,' finished the little widow, in a broken voice.

I said I was glad to hear it, for she evidently expected me to say something; and then I asked how long Dr. Hamilton had given him lessons in Latin and mathematics. She was only too ready to tell me, and seemed pleased at my interest.

'Ever since Nat hurt his arm in the railway accident—and I will say that Dr. Hamilton brought him round in a wonderful way; he found him at his books one evening, and ordered him off to bed in a hurry; but when he came next time he had a long talk with Nat, and promised to give him an hour when he could spare it. Sometimes Nat goes up to Gladwyn, but oftener Dr. Hamilton drops in here; he has taken a fancy to our kitchen, he says—but that is his way of putting it. There are plenty of folks who find fault with the Doctor, and say he is not what he ought to be to his own flesh and blood; but I always will have it, and Nathaniel says the same, that the Doctor has a fine character—why, Nat swears by him.'

I was beginning to be afraid that Mrs. Barton would never arrive at a full stop; she was a little like Mrs. Drabble in that; they were both discursive and parenthetical speakers, only Mrs. Drabble's meaning was more involved, but before I had time to answer a deep voice from the kitchen startled us.

'Mother, how long do you mean to keep Miss Garston in that cold, dark place? It is enough to starve her.' And at this rebuke Mrs. Barton hurried me into the front kitchen. I was tired by this time, and glad to bid them both good-night. And yet the widow's talk interested me. It was not Mr. Hamilton's fault that he had a face like a Romish priest; evidently he had his good points, like other people, in spite of his rudeness in laughing at me. But I could not; no, I could not tolerate that remark of his—'that a girl would do anything to make herself talked about.' It was odious; cynical; utterly malevolent. I hoped Uncle Max would defer the introduction as long as possible. I never wished to know anything of Gladwyn or its master. These thoughts occupied me until I fell asleep; and then I dreamt of Jill.

Once or twice I woke in the night, disturbed by a low growl from Tinker, who slept in the passage. I heard afterwards that his dreams were always haunted by cats. He was an inveterate enemy to all the feline species, with the exception of Peter, the great tabby cat. They had long ago sworn an armistice, and, in his way, Tinker took a great deal of notice of Peter.

It was strange to look round the low cottage room by the flickering, fast-dying firelight. The rain still pattered on the garden paths. I was rather dismayed to find that it had not ceased the next morning ; it is so pleasant to wake up in a fresh place and see the bright sunshine. This piece of good luck was denied me, however. When I looked out of my window I could only see dripping laurels and great pools in the gravel walks. The grey sky had not a break in it. I was glad when I was ready to go down to my parlour, for the fire and breakfast table would look cheerful by comparison ; and afterwards I would set to work so busily that I should not have time to notice the rain.

And so it proved ; for until my early dinner—or rather luncheon—was served, I was employed in unpacking and arranging my books and ornaments.

On my journeys to and fro I often paused at the low staircase window to reconnoitre the weather. There was no garden behind the cottage ; a small gravelled yard, where Mrs.

Barton kept her poultry and some rabbits belonging to Nathaniel, opened by a gate into a field. There was a cow-house there, and a white cow was standing rather disconsolately under some trees. I found out afterwards that both the field and the cow belonged to Mrs. Barton, so I could always rely on a good supply of sweet new milk.

Nathaniel had put up my bookshelves when I had sent them with the other furniture, so I had only to arrange the books. I made use, too, of some nails he had driven in for my pictures.

The parlour really looked very nice when I had finished; the new cream-coloured curtains were up, and I had tied them back with amber silk; two or three sunny little landscapes and Charlie's portrait, a beautifully painted photograph, hung on the walls; my favourite books were in their places, and the mantelpiece and the corner cupboards held some of the lovely old china that had belonged to mother. Aunt Philippa had wished me to leave it behind, as she feared it might be broken, but I liked to feast my eyes on the soft rich colours, and every piece was precious to me.

When I had disposed the furniture to the
best advantage—had placed my davenport
and work-table and special chair in the bow
window, and had replaced the shabby red
cloth by a handsome tapestry one, I called
Mrs. Barton to see the room.

She held up her hands in astonishment.

'Dear me, Miss Garston, it looks quite
a different place; what will Nathaniel say
when he sees it?—he is so fond of books and
pretty things—it only wants sunshine and a
bird-cage, and perhaps a geranium or two, to
make it quite a bower. May I make so bold,
ma'am, as to ask who that pleasant-faced young
gentleman is in the oak frame?'—but I think
she was sorry that she had asked the question
when I told her it was my twin-brother, now
in heaven.

'That is where my husband and my dear
little daughter both are,' she said, with moist
eyes, as she turned away from the picture. 'Oh,
there is a deal of trouble in the world, but you
are young to know it, ma'am,' and then she
looked kindly at me, and went away to give
Nathaniel his dinner.

CHAPTER VII.

GILES HAMILTON, ESQ.

T was quite late in the afternoon when I put the last finishing touches to my sitting-room, and it was already dusk when I left the cottage and walked quickly up the road that led to the Vicarage.

My busy day had not tired me, and I should have enjoyed a solitary ramble in spite of the wet roads and dark November sky, only I knew Uncle Max would be waiting for me. A keen sense of independence, of liberty, of congenial work in prospective, seemed to tingle in my veins, as though new life were coursing through them. I was no longer trammelled by the constant efforts to move in other people's grooves. I was free to think my own thought and lead my own life without reproof or hindrance.

The Vicarage was a red, irregular house, shut off from the road by a low wall, with a courtyard planted somewhat thickly with shrubs; the living rooms were chiefly at the back of the house, and their windows looked out on a pleasant garden; a glass door in the hall opened on a broad gravel terrace bordered by standard rose-trees, and beyond lay a smooth green lawn almost as level as a bowling-green; a laurel hedge divided it from an extensive kitchen garden, to which Uncle Max and Mr. Tudor devoted a great deal of their spare time and superfluous energies.

It was far too large a house for an unmarried man : the broad staircase and spacious rooms seemed to require the echo of children's voices. Uncle Max used to call it the barracks, but I think in his heart he liked the roomy emptiness; when he was restless he would prowl up and down the wide landing from one unused room to another. It was an old-fashioned house, and more than one generation had grown up in it. Uncle Max was fond of telling me about his predecessor's histories. Two little children had died in the big nursery overlooking the garden. There was a little brown room where a *ci-devant* vicar had written his sermons, with a big cupboard in the wall where he hung his cassock. He had a grown-up family, but his wife was dead. One day he married again and brought home a slim, pale-faced girl—a certain Priscilla Howe—to be the mistress of his house. There were stories rife in the village that her step-children were too much for poor, pretty Priscilla; that while her husband wrote his sermons in the little brown room, the young wife pined and moped in her green sitting-room.

Uncle Max found a picture of her one day in a garret where they stored apples; a faint musty smell clung to the canvas. 'Priscilla Howe' was written in one corner; there was a childish look on the small oval face; large melancholy eyes seemed appealing to one out of the canvas. She was dressed in a heavy white material like dimity, and held a few prim-roses between her fingers. What an innocent, pathetic little bride the stern-faced vicar must have brought home!

I read her epitaph afterwards when Uncle Max showed me her grave—'Priscilla, wife of Ralph Combermere, aged twenty, and her infant son'—what a sad little inscription! But Uncle

Max read something sadder still one day.
A letter in faded ink was found in a corner of
the same old garret, and the signature was
' Priscilla '; there was only one sentence legible
in the whole, and to whom it was written remained a mystery—' Trust me, dear love, that
I shall ever do my duty in spite of flaunts and
jeers and most unkindly looks; and if God
spares me health, which I cannot believe, He
may yet right me in the eyes that no longer
look at me with fondness.'

Poor Priscilla! so her husband had ceased to
love her. No wonder the poor child dwindled
and pined among ' the flaunts and jeers and
most unkindly looks ' of her step-children.
One could imagine her clasping her baby to
her sad heart as she closed her eyes to the bitter
misunderstanding of this life. ' Where the weary
are at rest'—they might have written those
words upon her tomb.

The thought of Priscilla used to haunt me
when I roamed about the passages on windy
days; the old garret especially seemed haunted
by her memory. Uncle Max once said to
me that he could have constructed a romance
out of her poor little history. ' She came from

a place called Ecclesbourne Hall,' he said, one day. 'She was an heiress; old Ralph Combermere knew what he was about when he transplanted the pale primrose. Do you know, Ursula, this room is supposed to be haunted? And one of the maids told me seriously that Mistress Combermere walks here on windy nights with her babe in her arms; fancy such a report in an English vicarage!'

When I reached the house the little maid who opened the door informed me that Uncle Max was in his study; it was a large room with a bay window overlooking the garden, and I knew Uncle Max never used any other room except for his meals. I had volunteered to announce myself. I was never formal with Max, so I knocked at the door and, without waiting to hear his voice in reply, marched in without ceremony.

But the next moment I stood discomfited on the threshold, for instead of Uncle Max's familiar face I saw a dark, closely cropped head bending over the table as though searching for something, and the ruddy firelight reflected the broad shoulders and hairless profile of the obnoxious Mr. Hamilton.

My first idea was to escape, and my fingers were already on the door handle when he turned abruptly and saw me. 'I beg your pardon,' coming towards me and speaking in the deep peculiar voice I had already heard. 'I was hunting for the matches that Cunliffe always mislays. You are Miss Garston, are you not? I was told to expect you;' and then he actually shook hands with me in an off hand way.

I am not generally devoid of presence of mind, but at that moment I behaved as awkwardly as a school-girl. If I could only have thought of some excuse for leaving him; an errand or a message to Mrs. Drabble; but no form of words would occur to me. I could only mutter an apology for my abrupt entrance, and ask after Uncle Max, stammering with confusion all the time, and then take the chair he was placing for me, while he renewed his search for the match-box.

'Oh, Cunliffe has only gone down to the village to post his letters—he will be back in a few minutes; ah! here are the matches. Now we shall be able to see each other,' and he coolly lighted Uncle Max's reading lamp and two candles, and stirred the fire with such a vigorous hand that the huge lump of coal splintered into fragments.

'There; I do like a mighty blaze—take that newspaper, Miss Garston, if the flame scorches your face. I know young ladies are afraid of their complexions.' Why need he have said that, as though my brown skin were Sara's pretty pink cheeks! 'Why do you not throw off your wraps if the room be too hot?' And he spoke so imperatively that I actually obeyed him, and got rid of my hat and ulster, which he deposited on the couch.

I did not like the look of Mr. Hamilton any better than I had liked it yesterday. His dark, smoothly shaven face was not to my taste—it looked stern and forbidding. He had a low forehead, and there was a hard set look about the mouth, and the eyes were almost disagreeable in their keenness.

Perhaps I was prejudiced, but he looked to me like a man who rarely laughed, and who would take a pleasure in saying bitter things; his voice was not unpleasant, but it had a peculiar depth in it, and now and then there was an odd break in it that was almost a hesitation.

'Well,' he said, looking full at me—but I

was sure, not in the least wishful to set me at my
ease; 'I suppose I ought to introduce myself.
My name is Hamilton.'

I bowed. I certainly did not think it
necessary that I should tell him that I was
aware of that fact.

'We met yesterday, when you were good
enough to put up with Nap's company. I was
half disposed to introduce myself then—only I
feared you would be shocked at such a piece of
unconventionality; young ladies have such
strict ideas of decorum.'

'And very properly so too,' I put in severely,
for my irritation was getting the better of my
nervousness. I could not bear the tone in which
he said 'young ladies.' I felt convinced he had
an antipathy to the whole sex.

'Our skies were very uncivil in their welcome,' he went on, quite disregarding my
remark; 'it was the wettest night we have had
for an age. I was quite savage when I found
the horses had been taken out of their warm
stables—the coachman was an ass, as I told
him.'

'You scolded him somewhat severely.'

'Ah, did you hear me?' smiling a little at

that, as though he were amused. 'I am afraid I speak my mind pretty freely, in spite of by-standers. Well, Miss Garston, so I hear you have come down as a sort of female Quixote among us. Heathfield is to be the scene of your mission.'

I was so angry at the tone in which he said this, that I made no reply. What right had a perfect stranger to meddle in my business?—it was all Uncle Max's fault; if he had only have held his tongue.

'Cunliffe was up at Gladwyn the other night,' he continued, in the same offhand way, ' and he told us all about it.'

'I am sorry to hear it,' very stiffly.

'Sorry—why? Good deeds ought to be talked about, ought they not, *pro bono publico*, eh—why not, Miss Garston ?'

'Good intentions are not deeds.'

'True, you have me there. I suppose you think you must not reckon on your chickens before they are hatched; the *pro bono publico* scheme is not properly hatched yet, except in theory. I am afraid I shall make you angry if I tell you I was rather amused at the whole thing.'

'I am glad to afford you amusement, Mr. Hamilton.'

'Ah, I see you are deeply offended; what a pity, and in five minutes too—that comes of my unfortunate habit of speaking my mind. Let me follow this out. I am afraid Cunliffe has been a traitor; that fellow is not reliable—no parsons are. Let me hear what you have against me, Miss Garston. I have spoken against your pet theory and you are aggrieved in consequence.'

He spoke in a half-jesting manner, but his ironical voice challenged me.

I felt I detested him; and he should know why.

'I expected to be misunderstood,' I returned coldly, 'but hardly to be accused of hysterical goodness. To be sure, a girl will do anything nowadays to get herself talked about!'

'Oh,' in a low voice, 'that rascal! but I will be even with him. How many more of my speeches did Cunliffe repeat?'

'Oh, I had heard enough,' I replied hastily. 'Does it not strike you as a little hard, Mr. Hamilton, that one should be judged beforehand in this harsh manner, that because some girls are full of vagaries, the whole sex must be condemned ? '

' Oh, if you put it in that cut-and-dried way, I must plead guilty ; in fact, I should owe you some sort of apology—only—' with a stress on the word—' my speech was not intended for the house-top. I am rather a sceptic about female missions, Miss Garston, and do not always measure my words when I am discussing abstract theories with a friend. In my opinion Cunliffe is the one you ought to blame, though if the speech rankles I will take my share.'

' I certainly wish you had not said it, Mr. Hamilton.'

' There, now '—in an injured voice—' that is the way you treat my handsome apology, and I am not a man ever to own myself in the wrong, mind you. What does it matter, may I ask, what I think of girls in the abstract ? I had not met you, Miss Garston, or discussed the subject in its bearings ; so where may the offence lie ? Of course you have no answer ready ; of course you have taken offence where none is meant. This is so like a woman—to undertake to renovate society, and lose her temper at the first adverse word.'

He was looking at me with a peculiar but not unkindly smile as he spoke; in fact, his expression was almost pleasant; but I was too much prejudiced to be softened. I did not care in the least what he thought of my temper; I was quite sure he had one of his own.

'No one likes to meet discouragement on the threshold,' I answered curtly.

'Not if it comes out with timbrels and dances, like Jephtha's daughter, to be sacrificed —that was discouragement on the threshold with a vengeance. I was always sorry for that old fellow. Well, *à propos* of that touching remark—which, by the way, is exquisitely feminine—supposing we strike a truce. I dare say you look upon me as an interfering stranger; but the fact is, I am the poor folks' doctor down here; so you cannot work without me. That alters the case, eh?'—with a smile meant to be propitiatory, but really too triumphant for my taste.

'Under those circumstances I could wish that you had less narrow views of women's work,' I returned with some warmth.

He opened his eyes so widely at this that
at any other moment I should have been
amused.

'By all that is wonderful, it is the first time
I have been accused of narrowness'—and here
he gave a gruff little laugh. 'I think I had
better leave you alone, Miss Garston, and label
you "dangerous." There is a hot sparkle in
your eyes that warns me to keep off the premises. "Trespassers will be taken up." I
begin to feel uncomfortable. Cunliffe has put
me *en parole*, and I dare not break bounds.
Can you manage to sit in the same room a
little longer with such a heretic?'

'Heretics can be converted.'

He shrugged his shoulders at this.

'Not such a hardened sceptic as myself.
Now, look here, Miss Garston. I will say
something civil. I believe you are in earnest;
so it shall be *pax* between us; and I will promise not to thwart you. As for women's mission
in general, I believe their principal mission is
not to stop at home and mind their own business; in fact, home and homely duties are the
last straws that break the back of the emanci-
pated woman.' And with these audacious words

Mr. Hamilton stirred the fire again with prodigious energy. Happily Uncle Max came into the room at that moment; so I was spared any reply.

Max must have thought that I was suspiciously glad to see him, for he looked from one to the other rather anxiously.

'Sorry to be so late, Ursula; but I met Pardoe, and he entrapped me into an argument. Well, how have you and my friend Hamilton got on together?'

I turned away without answering, but Mr. Hamilton responded in a melancholy voice —

'I have been suppressed, like the dormouse in Alice's teapot. There is very little left of me. I had no idea your niece had such a taste for argument, Cunliffe. I take it rather unkindly that I was not warned off the track.'

'So you two have been quarrelling'—and Uncle Max looked a little vexed. 'What a fellow you are, Hamilton, for stroking a person the wrong way. Of course Ursula has believed all your cross-grained remarks?'

'Swallowed them whole and entire; and a fit of moral indigestion is the result. Well, I must be going; but first let me administer a palliative, Miss Garston. What time do you have breakfast? If it be before ten, I shall be happy to introduce you to a very eligible case.'

I would have given much to have dispensed with Mr. Hamilton's patronage; but under the circumstances it would have been absurd to have refused his offer. I could not sacrifice my work to my temper; but I recognised with a sinking heart that Mr. Hamilton would cross my daily path. The idea was as delightful to me as the anticipation of a daily east wind. I refrained myself, however, and briefly mentioned that I would be ready by nine.

' Oh, that is an hour too early; I will call for you at ten. Let me see, you are at the White Cottage. You are not curious about your first patient; in that you are not a true daughter of Eve. Well, good-bye, Miss Garston; good-bye, Cunliffe.' And he left the room without shaking hands with me again.

Uncle Max followed him out into the hall, and they stood so long talking that I lost patience, and went into the kitchen to see Mrs. Drabble.

She received me in a resigned way, as usual, and talked without taking breath once while she buttered the hot cakes and prepared the tea-tray. I understood her to say that Mr. Tudor's collars were her chief cares in life; that no young gentleman she had ever known was so hard to please in the matter of starch; that her master was a lamb in comparison; and did I not think he was looking ill and overworking himself?

I had some difficulty in finding out to whom she was alluding, but I imagined she meant her master, who was certainly looking a little thin, and then she went off on another tack.

'Folks seem mighty curious about you, Miss Ursula; people do say that only a young lady crossed in love would think of doing such an out-of-the-way thing as putting up at the White Cottage, and nursing poor people. There was Rebecca Saunders — you knew Rebecca at the Post Office—she said to me last night, "So your young lady has come, Mrs. Drabble; the Vicar was at the station, I hear, and Dr. Hamilton came down by the same train—wasn't that curious now? I am thinking she must be a mighty independent sort of person to take this work on her; there has been trouble somewhere, take my word for it, for it is not in young folks' nature to go in for work and no play." '

'Oh, I mean to play as well as work,' I returned, laughing. 'Don't tell me any more, Mrs. Drabble; people will talk in a village, but I would rather not hear what they say.' And then I went back to the study and made tea for Uncle Max, and tried to pretend that I felt quite myself, and was not the least uneasy in my mind, as though I would deceive Max.

'Well, Ursula,' he said, shaking his head at me, 'did Hamilton or Mrs. Drabble give you those hot cheeks?'

'Oh, Uncle Max,' I returned hastily, 'I am so sorry Mr. Hamilton is your friend.'

'Why so, little She-Bear?'

'Because—because—I detest him; he is the most disagreeable, insufferable, domineering person I have ever met.'

'Candid; but then you were always outspoken, my dear. Now, shall I tell you what this disagreeable, insufferable, domineering person said to me in the hall?'

'Oh, nothing he said will make any difference to my opinion, I assure you.'

'Possibly not, but it is too good to be lost He said : " That little girl actually believes in herself and her work ; it is quite refreshing to meet with such *naïveté* nowadays. Ursula did you call her? Well, the name just suits her ;" how do you like that, poor little bear ?'

'I like it as well as I liked all Mr. Hamilton's speeches. Max, do you really care for that odious man? Must I be civil to him ?'

'Indeed, I hope you will be civil, Ursula,' replied Uncle Max, in an alarmed voice. 'My dear, Giles Hamilton, Esq. is my most influential parishioner; he is rich ; he doctors all my poor people *gratis*; bullies them one moment, and does them a good turn in the next ; he is clever, kind-hearted, and has no end of good points, and though he is eccentric and has plenty of faults, we chum together excellently, and I am very intimate with his people.'

'His people—who are they ?' I asked irritably.

'Oh, it is a queer household up at Gladwyn,' returned Max, rather uneasily. 'Hamilton has a cousin living with him as well as his two sisters ; her name is Darrell—Etta

Darrell; she is a stylish-looking woman, about five-and-thirty; one never knows a lady's age exactly.'

'Are his sisters very young, then? Does Miss Darrell manage the house?'

'Yes—how could you guess that?' looking at me in surprise. 'Gladys, Miss Hamilton, is about three-and-twenty, but she is very delicate; the younger one, Elizabeth, is two years younger; they are Hamilton's half-sisters —his father married twice—that accounts for a good deal.'

'How do you mean—accounts for a good deal, Max?'

'Why, people say that Hamilton doesn't always get on with his sisters,' he returned reluctantly; 'there are often misunderstandings in families—want of harmony, and that sort of thing; mind, I do not say it is true.'

'But you are so often at Gladwyn, you ought to know, Max.'

'Yes, of course; and now and then I have seen Hamilton a little stern with his sisters; he is rather irritable by nature. I don't quite understand things myself, but I have got it into my head that they would be happier without

Miss Darrell; she is a splendid manager, but it puts Miss Hamilton out of her right place.'

'But she is an invalid, you say?'

'No, not an invalid, only very delicate, and a little morbid; not quite what a girl ought to be. You could do some good there, Ursula,' rather eagerly. 'Miss Hamilton has no friends of her own age; she is reserved—peculiar. You might be a comfort to her; you are sympathetic—sensible, and have known trouble yourself. I should like to see you use your influence there.'

'I will try, if you wish it, Max; and her name is Gladys?'

'Yes, Gladys, of Gladwyn,' he returned with a smile, but I thought he said it with rather a singular intonation, but it had a musical sound, and I repeated it again to myself—'Gladys, of Gladwyn.'

CHAPTER VIII.

NEW BROOMS SWEEP CLEAN.

E were interrupted just then by Mrs.
Drabble, who came in for the tea
things, and as usual held a long col-
loquy with her master on sundry domestic
affairs. When she had at last withdrawn,
Uncle Max did not resume the subject—I was
somewhat disappointed at this, and in spite of
my strong antipathy to Mr. Hamilton I wanted
to hear more about his sisters.

He disregarded my hints, however, and
began talking to me about my work.

'Do you know anything about the family
Mr. Hamilton mentioned?' I asked rather
eagerly.

'Oh, yes; Mary Marshall's is a very sad

case ; she has seven children, not one of them old enough to work for himself; and she is dying, poor creature, of consumption. Her husband is a navvy, and he is at work at Lewes ; I believe he is pretty steady, and sends the greater part of his wages to his wife, but there are too many mouths to feed to allow of comforts ; his old blind mother lives with them. I believe the neighbours are kind and helpful, and Peggy, the eldest child, is a sharp little creature, but you can imagine the miserable condition of such a home.'

'Yes, indeed,' and I shuddered as I recalled many a sad scene in my father's home.

'I have sent in a woman once or twice to clean up the place ; and Mrs. Drabble has made excellent beef-tea, but the last lot turned sour from being left in the hot kitchen one night, and the cat upset the basin of calf's-foot jelly—at least, the children said so. I go there myself, because Tudor says the air of the place turns him sick—he looked as white as a ghost after his last visit, and declared he was poisoned with foul air.'

'I dare say he was right, Max ; poor people have such an objection to open their windows.'

'I believe you there. I have talked myself nearly hoarse on that subject. Hamilton and I propose giving lectures in the schoolroom on domestic hygiene. There is a fearful want of sanitary knowledge in women belonging to the lower class ; want of cleanliness, want of ventilation, want of white-washing, are triple evils that lead to the most lamentable results—we cannot get people to understand the common laws of life; the air of their rooms may be musty, stagnant, and corrupt, and yet they are astonished if their children have an attack of scarlet fever or diphtheria.'

I commended the notion of the lectures warmly, and asked with whom the idea had originated.

'Oh, Hamilton, of course—he is the moving spirit of everything ; we have planned the whole thing out. There is to be a lecture every Friday evening ; the first is to be on household hygiene, the sanitary condition of houses, ventilation, cleanliness, &c. In the second lecture Hamilton will speak of the laws of health, self-management, personal cleanliness, to be followed by a few simple lectures on nursing, sick cookery, and the treatment of infantile diseases. We want

all the mothers to attend.   Do you think it a
good idea, Ursula?'

'It is an excellent one,' I returned reluctantly, for I grudged the praise to Mr. Hamilton.
He could benefit his fellow-creatures, and give
time and strength and energy to the poor sick
people, and yet sneer at me civilly when I
wanted to do the same, just because I was a
woman.   Perhaps Max was disappointed with
my want of enthusiasm, for he ceased talking
of the lectures, and said he had some more
letters to write before dinner, and during the
rest of the evening, though we discussed a
hundred different topics, Mr. Hamilton's name
was not again mentioned.

Uncle Max walked with me to the gate of the
White Cottage, and bade me a cheerful good-
night.

'I like to feel you are near me, Ursula,'
he said quite affectionately ; 'an old bachelor
like myself gets into a groove, and the society
of a vigorous young woman, brimful of philan-
thropy and crotchets, will rub me up and do me
good ; one goes to sleep sometimes,' he finished
rather mournfully, and then he walked away
in the darkness, and I stood for a minute to
watch him.

It seemed to me that Max was a little different this evening. He was always kind, always cheerful, he never wrapped himself up in gloomy reserve like other people, however depressed or ill at ease he might be; but Mrs. Drabble was right—he was certainly thinner, and there was an anxious careworn look about his face when he was not speaking. I was certain too that his cheerfulness and ready flow of conversation were not without effort. I had asked him once if he were quite well, and he had looked at me in evident astonishment.

'Perfectly well, thank you, in a state of rude health—nothing ever ails me; why do you ask?' But I evaded this question, for I knew Max hated to be watched—and after all what right had I to intrude into his private anxieties? doubtless he had plenty of these like other men. The management of a large parish was on his shoulders, he was too conscientious and hard-working to spare himself; but somehow the shadow lying deep down in Max's honest brown eyes haunted me as I unlatched the cottage door.

I heard Nathaniel's voice in the kitchen, and went in to bid him and his mother good-

night. Mrs. Barton was not there, however,
but to my chagrin Mr. Hamilton occupied her
seat ; he looked up with rather a quizzical glance
as I entered—he and Nathaniel had the round
table between them, strewn with books and
papers ; Nathaniel was writing, and Mr. Hamilton was sitting opposite to him.

' I beg your pardon,' I said hurriedly, ' I
thought Mrs. Barton was here.'

' She has gone to bed,' returned Mr.
Hamilton, coolly ; ' my friend Nathaniel and I
are hard at work, as you see. Do you know anything of mathematics, Miss Garston—no, you
shake your head——' I do not know what
more he would have said, but I escaped with
a quick good-night.

As I went upstairs I made a resolution to
avoid the kitchen in future. I might at any
moment stumble upon Mr. Hamilton. I had
forgotten that he gave Nathaniel lessons sometimes in the evening—what an ubiquitous
mortal this man appeared : here, there, and
everywhere ! It had given me rather a shock
to see him so comfortably domiciled in Mrs.
Barton's cosy kitchen ; he looked as much at
home there as in Uncle Max's study. How

bright Nathaniel had looked as he raised his head to bid me good-night! I was obliged to confess that they had seemed as happy as possible.

It was very late when he left the cottage; I was just sinking off to sleep when I heard his voice under my window. Tinker heard it too and barked, and then the gate shut with a sudden sharp click and all was still. Nathaniel must have crept up to bed in his stocking-feet, as they say in some parts, for I never heard him pass my door.

I was glad to be greeted by sunshine the next morning; the day seemed to smile on my new work like an unuttered benison as I went down to my solitary breakfast. I resolved that nothing Mr. Hamilton could say should damp or put me out of temper, and then I sat down and read a sad rambling letter from Jill, which was so quaint and original, in spite of its lugubriousness, that it made me smile.

I was standing by the door caressing Tinker, who was in a frolicking mood this morning, when I saw Mr. Hamilton cross the road; he wore a dark tweed suit and a soft felt hat—a costume that did not suit him in the least ; he held open the gate for me, and made a sign that I should join him.   As I approached without hurrying myself in the least he looked inquiringly at the basket I carried.

'I hope you do not intend to pauperise your patients,' was his first greeting.

'Oh, no,' was my reply, but I did not volunteer any information as to the contents of the basket.   There was certainly a jar of beef-tea that Mrs. Drabble had given me, and a few grapes ; but the little store of soap, soda, fine rags, and the two or three clean towels and cloths would have surprised him a little, though he might have understood the meaning of the neat housewife.

'I am glad you wear print dresses,' was his next remark ; 'they are proper for a nurse—stuff gowns that do not wash are abominations. I am taking you to a very dirty place, Miss Garston, but what can you expect when there are seven children under thirteen years of age and the mother is dying ?   She was a clean capable body when she was up—it is hard for her to see the place like a pig-sty now. Old Mrs. Marshall is blind, and is as helpless as the children.' He spoke abruptly, but not without feeling.

'The neighbours are good to them, Uncle Max tells me?'

'Oh, yes; they come in and tidy up a bit —that is their expression; now and then they wash the baby or take off a batch of dirty clothes, but they have their own homes and children. I tell my patient that she would be far more comfortable in a hospital; but she says she cannot leave the children, she would rather die at home. That is what they all say.'

'But the poor creatures mean what they say, Mr. Hamilton.'

'Oh, but it is all nonsense!' he returned irritably. She can do nothing for the children, she cannot have a moment's quiet or a moment's comfort with all those grimy noisy creatures rushing in and out. I found her sitting up in bed yesterday, in danger of breaking a blood-vessel through coughing, because one of the imps had fallen down and cut his head and she was trying to plaster it.'

'Her husband ought to be with her,' I said somewhat indignantly.

'He is on a job somewhere, and cannot

come home ; they must have bread to eat, and he must work. This is the house,' pointing to a low white cottage at the end of a long straggling street of similar houses; two or three untidy-looking children were playing in the front garden with some oyster-shells and a wooden horse without a head. One little white-headed urchin clapped his hands when he saw Mr. Hamilton, and a pretty little girl with a very dirty·face ran up to him and clasped him round the knee.

' 'As oo' any pennies to-day?' she lisped.

'No nonsense; run away, children,' he said in a rough voice that did not in the least alarm them, for they scampered after us into the porch until an elder girl, with a year-old baby in her arms, met us on the threshold and scolded them away.

Mr. Hamilton shook a big stick at them.

'I shall give no pennies to children with dirty faces. Well, Peggy, how is mother? Have the boys gone to school, both of them? That is right. This is the lady who is coming to look after mother.'

Here Peggy dropped a curtsy and said, 'Yes, sir,' and 'yes please, mum.'

'Mind you do all she tells you; now out of my way. I want to speak to your grandmother a moment, and then I will come into the other room.'

I followed him into the untidy, miserable-looking kitchen. An old woman was sitting by the fire with an infant in her arms; we found out that it belonged to the neighbour who was washing out some things in the yard. She came in by-and-by, clattering over the stones in her thick clogs—a brisk, untidy-looking young woman—and looked at me curiously as she took her baby.

'I must be going home now, Granny,' she said, in a loud, good-humoured voice. 'Peggy can rinse out the few things I've left.'

Granny had a pleasant, weather-beaten face, only it looked sunken and pale, and the poor blind eyes had a pathetic, unseeing look in them. To my surprise she looked neat and clean. I had yet to learn the slow martyrdom the poor soul had endured during the last few months in that squalid, miserable household. To her cleanliness was next to godliness. She had brought up a large family well and thriftily, and now in her old age and helplessness her

life had no comfort in it. I was rather surprised to see Mr. Hamilton shake the wrinkled
hand heartily.

'Well, Elspeth, what news of your son?
Is he likely to come home soon?'

'Nay, Doctor,' in a faint old treble;
'Andrew cannot leave his job for two or three
months to come. He is terrible down-hearted
about poor Mary. Ay, she has been a good
wife to him and the bairns; but look at her
now! Poor thing, poor thing.'

'We must all dree our weird. You are a
canny Scotchwoman and know what that means.
Come, you must cheer up, for I have brought a
young lady with me who is going to put your
daughter-in-law a little more comfortable and
see after her from time to time.'

'Ay, but that is cheering news,' returned
Elspeth; and one of the rare tears of old age
stole down her withered cheek. 'My poor
Mary; she is patient, and never complains;
but the good Lord is laying a heavy cross on
her.'

'That is true,' muttered Mr. Hamilton, and
then he said in a businesslike tone—'Now
for the patient, Miss Garston;' and as he led

the way across the narrow passage we could hear the hard, gasping cough of the sick woman.

Peggy, with the baby still in her arms, was trying to stir a black, cindery fire, that was filling the room with smoke. The child was crying, and the poor invalid was sitting up in bed nearly suffocated by her cough. The great four-post bed blocked up the little window. The remains of a meal were still on the big round table. Some clothes were drying by the hearth ; a thin tortoise-shell cat was licking up a stream of milk that was filtering slowly across the floor, in the midst of jugs, cans, a broken broom, some children's toys, and two or three boots. The bed looked as though it had not been made for days—the quilt and valance were deplorably dirty ; but the poor creature herself looked neat and clean, and her hair was drawn off from her sunken cheeks and knotted carefully at the back of her head. Mr. Hamilton uttered an exclamation of impatience when he saw the smoke, and almost snatched the poker out of Peggy's hands.

'Take the child away,' he said angrily. 'Miss Garston, if you can find some paper and wood in this infernal confusion, I shall be obliged to you ; this smoke must be stopped.'

I found the broken lid of a box that split up like tinder, and Peggy brought me an old newspaper, and then I stood by while Mr. Hamilton skilfully manipulated the miserable fire.

' All these ashes must be removed,' he said curtly, as he rose with blackened hands ; ' the whole fireplace is blocked up with them.' And then he went to the pump and washed his hands, while I sent Peggy after him with a nice clean towel from my basket. While he was gone I stepped up to the bed and said a word or two to poor Mrs. Marshall.

She must have been a comely creature in her days of health, but she was fearfully wasted now. The disease was evidently running its course ; as she lay there exhausted and panting, I knew her lease of life would not be long.

' It was the smoke,' she panted. ' Peggy is young ; she muddles over the fire. Last night it went out, and she was near an hour getting it to light.'

' It is burning beautifully now, ' I returned, and then Mr. Hamilton came back and began to examine his patient professionally. I was

surprised to find that his abrupt manner left
him ; he spoke to Mrs. Marshall so gently, and
with such evident sympathy, that I could hardly
believe it was the same person—her wan face
seemed to light up with gratitude ; but when
he turned to me to give some directions for
her treatment he spoke with his old dryness.

'I shall be here about the same time to-
morrow,' he finished ; and then he nodded to
us both, and went away.

'Mrs. Marshall,' I said, as I warmed the beef-
tea with some difficulty in a small broken pip-
kin, 'do you know of any strong capable girl
who would clean up the place a little for me ? '

'There is Weatherley's eldest girl Hope still
at home,' she replied, after a moment's hesitation, 'but her mother will not let her work
without pay. She is a poor sort of neighbour,
is Susan Weatherley, and is very niggardly in
helping people.'

'Of course I should pay Hope,' I answered
decidedly ; and when the beef-tea was ready I
called Peggy and sent her on my errand. One
glance at the place showed me that I could do
nothing for my patient without help. Happily
I had seen some sheets drying by the kitchen

fire, but they would hardly be ready for us
before the evening; but when Mrs. Marshall
had taken her beef-tea I covered her up and
tried to smooth the untidy quilt. Then telling
her that we were going to make her room a
little more comfortable, I pinned up my dress
and enveloped myself in a holland apron ready
for work.

Peggy came back at this moment with a
big, strapping girl of sixteen, who looked strong
and willing. She was evidently not a woman
of words, but she grinned cheerful acquiescence
when I set her to work on the grate, while I
cleared the table and carried out all the miscel-
laneous articles that littered the floor.

Mrs. Marshall watched us with astonished
eyes. ' Oh dear! oh dear!' I heard her say to
herself, ' and a lady too!' but I took no notice.

I sent Hope once or twice across to her
mother for various articles we needed—black-
lead, a scrubbing-brush, some house-flannel and
soft soap—and when she had finished the grate
I set her to scrub the floor, as it was black with
dirt. I was afraid of the damp boards for my
patient, but I covered her up as carefully as
possible, and pinned some old window cur-

tains across the bed. Neglect and want of cleanliness had made the air of the sick room so fœtid and poisonous that one could hardly breathe it with safety.

Now and then I looked in the other room and spoke a cheerful word to Granny. Peggy was doing her best for the children, but the poor baby seemed very fretful. Towards noon two rough-headed boys made their appearance and began clamouring for their dinner. The same untidy young woman whom I had seen before came clattering up the yard again in her clogs and helped Peggy spread great slices of bread and treacle for the hungry children, and warmed some food for the baby. I saw Granny trying to eat a piece of bread and dripping that they gave her and then lay it down without a word; no wonder her poor cheeks were so white and sunken.

Mrs. Drabble had promised me some more beef-tea, so I warmed a cupful for Granny and broke up a slice of stale bread in it; it was touching to see her enjoyment of the warm food. The eldest boy, Tim, was nearly eleven years old and looked a sharp little fellow, so I set him to clean up the kitchen with Peggy and make things a little tidier, and promised some buns to all the children who had clean faces and hands at tea-time.

I left Hope still at work when I went up to the White Cottage to eat some dinner. Mrs. Barton had made a delicate custard-pudding, which I carried off for the invalid's and Granny's supper. My young healthy appetite needed no tempting, and my morning's work had only whetted it. I did not linger long in my pretty parlour, for a heavy task was before me. I was determined the sick room should have a different appearance the next morning.

I sent Hope to her dinner while I washed and made my patient comfortable. The room felt fresher and sweeter already; a bright fire burned in the polished grate; Hope had scoured the table and wiped the chairs, and the dirty quilt and valance had been sent to Mrs. Weatherley's to be washed. When Hope returned, and the sheets were aired, we re-made the bed. I had sent a message early to Mrs. Drabble begging for some of the lending blankets and a clean coloured quilt, which she had sent down by a boy. The scarlet cover looked so warm and snug that I stood still to admire the effect;

poor Mary fairly cried when I laid her back on her pillow.

'It feels all so clean and heavenly,' she sobbed; 'it is just a comfort to lie and see the room.'

'I mean Granny to come and have her tea here,' I said, for I was longing for the dear old woman to have her share of some of the comfort; and I had just led her in and put her in the big shiny chair by the fire, when Uncle Max put his head in and looked at us.

'Just so,' he said, nodding his head, and a pleased expression came into his eyes. 'Bravo, Ursula! Tudor won't know the place again. How you must have worked, child!' and then he came in and talked to the sick woman.

I had taken a cup of tea standing, for I was determined not to go home and rest until I left for the night. I could not forget the poor fretful baby, and, indeed, all the children were miserably neglected. I made up my mind that Hope and I would wash the poor little creatures and put them comfortably to bed. My first day's work was certainly exceptionally hard, but it would make my future work easier.

The baby was a pale, delicate little creature,

very backward for its age; it left off fretting
directly I took it in my lap, and began staring
at me with its large blue eyes. Hope had just
filled the large tub, and the children were
crowding round it with evident amusement,
when Uncle Max came in. He contemplated
the scene with twinkling eyes.

'"There was an old woman who lived in
a shoe,"' he began humorously. 'My dear
Ursula, do you mean to say you are going to
wash all those children? the tub looks suggestive, certainly.'

I nodded.

'Who would have believed in such an
overplus of energy? hard work certainly agrees
with you,' and then he went out laughing, and
we set to work, and then Hope and I carried
in the children by detachments that the poor
mother might see the clean rosy faces. I am
afraid we had to bribe Jock, the youngest boy,
for he evidently disliked soap and water.

Peggy and the baby slept in the mother's
room; there was a little bed in the corner for
them. I did not leave until Granny had been
taken upstairs, and poor tired Peggy was fast
asleep with the baby beside her.

The room looked so comfortable when I turned for a last peep. I had drawn the round table to the bed, and left the night-light and cooling drink beside the sick woman; she was propped up with pillows and her breathing seemed easier. When I bade her good-night, and told her I should be round early in the morning, she said: 'Then it will be the first morning I shall not dread to wake. Thank you kindly, dear Miss, for all you have done,' and her soft brown eyes looked at me gratefully.

CHAPTER IX.

THE FLAG OF TRUCE.

T could not be denied that I was extremely tired as I walked down the dark road; but in spite of fatigue my heart felt lighter than it had done since Charlie's death, and the warm glow from the window of my little parlour seemed to welcome me, it looked so snug and bright. My low chair was drawn to the fire, a sort of tea-supper was awaiting me, and Mrs. Barton came out of the kitchen as soon as I had lifted the latch to ask what she could do for me.

The first words surprised me greatly. Mr. Hamilton had called late in the afternoon, and had seemed somewhat surprised to hear I was still at the cottage, but he had left no message, and Mrs. Barton had no idea what he wanted with me.

I was half inclined to think that he had another case ready for me, but I had done my day's work and refused to think of the morrow. The first volume of 'Kingsley's Life' was lying on the little table, I had brought it from the Vicarage the preceding evening. I passed a delicious hour in my luxurious chair, and went to bed reluctantly that I might be fit for the next day's fatigue.

As soon as I had breakfasted the next morning and read my letters, a chatty one from Sara, and an affectionate note from Lesbia, I went down to the cottage.

I found my patient a little easier ; she had passed a better night, and seemed on the whole more cheerful. Hope had arrived, and was scrubbing the kitchen as I had enjoined her ; baby seemed poorly and fretful. I gave her in charge of Peggy and set myself to the work of putting my patient and the sick room in order, after which I intended to wash the baby and see after Granny's and the children's dinner.

I had just brushed up the hearth and put the kettle to boil, when Mr. Hamilton's shadow crossed the window, and the next moment he was in the room.

I was sure that a half smile of approbation came to his lips as he looked round the room; he lifted his eyebrows as though in surprise as he noticed everything—the neat hearth, white boards, and bright window, and lastly the comfortable appearance of the bed with its scarlet quilt and clean sheets.

'This is quite a transformation scene, Miss Garston,' he said, in an approving tone. 'No wonder you were not at home in the afternoon; my patient looks cheery too, one would think I had set the fairy Order to work.' I felt that this was meant for high praise, and I received it graciously. I knew 1 had worked well and achieved wonders; but then I had Hope's strong arms to help me—it had been straightforward work, too, with no complication, any charwoman could have done it as well. I was sorry that his commendation set Mrs. Marshall's tongue going; she became so voluble in spite of her cough, that I was obliged to enforce silence.

Mr. Hamilton's visit was very brief. I asked him to prescribe for the baby, but he said nothing ailed it in particular—it had always been sickly, and had been so neglected of late, most likely sour food had been given it. Mrs. Tyler, the next door neighbour, who had looked after it, was a thoughtless body. 'You must take it in hand yourself, Miss Garston,' he finished; ' keep it warm and clean and see the food properly prepared, that will be better than any medicine,' and then he went off with his usual abruptness, only I saw him stop at the gate to give pennies to Janie and little Jock.

There was still so much to do that I determined to spend the whole day at the cottage. I sent off all the dirty things for Mrs. Tyler to wash at home, for she was so noisy and untidy that I did not care to have her on the premises, and I thought Granny could sit in Mrs. Marshall's room and hold baby while Peggy waited on me and ran errands.

Hope worked splendidly; when she had scoured the kitchen and front passage, she went upstairs and scrubbed the two rooms where Granny and the children slept. I had made a potato pie with some scraps of meat Peggy had brought from the butcher's, and had seen the dish emptied by the hungry children. When I had fed the sandy cat and had had my own dinner, which Mrs. Barton had packed in a nice clean basket, and had peeped at my patient, I went upstairs to help Hope, and Peggy went with me. The state of the sleeping-rooms had horrified me in the morning; the windows had evidently not been open for weeks, the sheets on Granny's bed were black with dirt. Hope had washed the bedstead, and Peggy had lighted a fire, that the room might be habitable by night. Tim came up while we were busy, and stared at us. I was helping Peggy drag the mattresses and bed-clothes into the passage. The open windows and the wet boards reeking with soft soap evidently astonished him.

'Where be us to sleep to-night?' quoth Tim; 'it is colder than in the yard;' but Peggy, who was excited by her work, bade him hold his tongue and not stand gaping there blocking up the passage.

I had been singing over my work just to put heart into all of us, and make us forget what a very disagreeable business it was, when Tim again made his appearance and said there was a gentleman in the kitchen. 'He thought he knowed him, but wasn't sure, but he had asked for the lady.' I went down at once and found it was Mr. Tudor; he was sitting very comfortably by the fire with all the children round him; little Janie was on his knee, her face was clean and her pretty curls had been nicely brushed, so I did not mind her cuddling up to him, and I knew he was fond of children and always ready to play with them.

He put her down and shook hands with me, and said the Vicar had sent him to look after me as he could not come himself. I thought he looked a little amused at my appearance; and no wonder. I had quite forgotten that I had tied a handkerchief over my head to keep the dust from off my hair; with my holland bib-apron and sleeves, and pinned-up dress, I must have looked an odd figure; but when I said so he laughed, and observed that he rather admired my novel costume—it reminded him of a Highland peasant he had once seen.

'Was that you who were singing just now, Miss Garston?' he asked presently, looking at me with some attention.

'Yes,' I returned. 'You seem surprised; surely you have heard me sing at Hyde Park Gate?' But he shook his head very decidedly.

'I should not have forgotten your voice if
I had once heard it,' he said, in such a pleasant
manner that the straightforward compliment
did not embarrass me. 'You ought not to let
such a talent rust, Miss Garston; the Vicar
must utilise you for our Penny Readings.'

I was horrified at this notion, and told him
very seriously that nothing would induce me to
sing on a platform, but that it was not my
intention to let it rust, only I had my own
ideas how best to utilise it.

He looked curious at this, but I changed
the subject by asking him if he would like to
see Mrs. Marshall. He hesitated, coloured
slightly as though the question were distasteful,
then he put down Janie from his knee—for the
child had clambered up again—and said the
Vicar had undertaken the case as he was rather
new to the work, but he would see her if I
wished it.

I was provoking enough to say that I
did wish it, for I wanted him to see the comfortable appearance of the room that he so
dreaded to enter. I felt sorry for Mr. Tudor
in my heart that his work should be so distasteful to him; he was a fine, manly young

fellow, who would have made a splendid sailor or soldier, but sick rooms and old women were not to his taste, and yet he was very gentle and sympathising in his manners, and all the poor people liked him.

Granny was dozing by the fire, and the baby was asleep on the mother's bed, and as I opened the door I quite enjoyed Mr. Tudor's start of astonishment at the changed scene. I did not let him stay long, but I thought his kind looks and pleasant voice would cheer poor Mary. He said very little either to her or Elspeth, but what he said was sensible and to the point.

I sent him away after this, for my work was waiting for me. He went off laughing, and protesting that he had no idea that I had taken up the *rôle* of a charitable charwoman, and that the Vicar would remonstrate with me on the subject.

I think we all felt the brighter for Mr. Tudor's little visit, though he had said nothing specially clever; but he was an honest, genial creature, and I liked him thoroughly. I stopped at the cottage late that evening, for Mrs. Marshall wanted a letter written to her husband, and I could not refuse to do it. I was almost too tired to enjoy Kingsley that night, and found myself dozing over it, so I shut it up and went to bed.

Mr. Hamilton did not make his appearance until later the next day, when I was presiding over the children's dinner. I had just carried in a plate of lentil soup to Granny, whom I now kept entirely in the sick room, as she was too old to bear the children's noise, and the constant draughts from the opening door would soon have laid her on a sick bed. I had baby in my lap, and was feeding her when he looked in on us.

I rose at once to follow him into the sick room, but he waved me back.

'Do not disturb yourself, Miss Garston; you all look very comfortable. Jock, are you trying to swallow that spoon? You will find it a hard morsel.' And then he went into the other room, and, to my surprise, we did not see him again.

I left a little earlier that evening, as I knew Uncle Max meant to pay me a visit; but it was already dark when I closed the little gate behind me. I had not gone many paces when

I heard footsteps behind me, and, somewhat to my dismay, Mr. Hamilton joined me.

'Have you only just finished your day's work?' he said, in evident surprise. 'This will never do, Miss Garston; we shall have you knocking yourself up if you use up your time and strength so recklessly, and I want you for another case.'

'I am quite prepared for that,' I answered; but I am afraid my voice was a little weary. 'You called on me yesterday, Mr. Hamilton. I was sorry to be out, but there was so much to do that I stayed at the cottage until quite late in the evening.'

'Just so,' in rather a vexed tone. 'The village nurse will be on a sick bed herself if this goes on.'

'Oh, what nonsense!' I returned, laughing, for I forgot for the moment in the darkness that I was speaking to the formidable Mr. Hamilton. 'I do not always mean to work quite so hard. Mr. Tudor called me a charitable charwoman last evening; but this is an exceptional case—so many helpless beings, and such shocking mismanagement and neglect. When I put things on a proper footing I shall not spend so much time there.'

'What do you mean by putting things on a proper footing?' he asked, with some show of interest.

'When the place has been properly cleaned it will be kept tolerably tidy with less labour. Hope Weatherley has been hard at work for two days, and things are now pretty comfortable.'

'I suppose—excuse me if the question seems impertinent—but I imagine that you paid Hope out of your own purse?'

'For those two days certainly; it was necessary for my own comfort, speaking selfishly, that the place should be made habitable. My nursing would have been a mere mockery unless we could have got rid of the dirt.'

'You are perfectly right. I had no idea you were such a practical person, but if you will allow me to give you a hint—Marshall earns good wages—there ought to be sufficient money to pay for a moderate amount of help.'

'I told Mrs. Marshall so this morning,' I returned, pleased to find myself talking with such ease to Mr. Hamilton; but he seemed quite different to-night; evidently his *brusquerie* was a mere mannerism that he laid aside at

times; he had lost that sneering manner that I
so much disliked. I remembered Uncle Max
said that he was kind-hearted and eccentric.

' We had a long talk,' I went on. ' Marshall
sends the money regularly, and I am to manage
it. Mrs. Tyler is to wash for us, and I think
we can afford to have Hope for at least an hour
a day, to do the rough work—Peggy is so little
to do everything.'

' Heaven help poor Peg!' he ejaculated;
' for she will soon have all those children on
her hands. Mrs. Marshall cannot last long.
Well, Miss Garston, how many hours do you
intend to spend at the cottage daily?'

' I should think two hours in the morning,
and an hour and a half in the late afternoon
or evening might do, unless there be a change
for the worse, or Elspeth falls ill—she is very
old and feeble.'

' She was half starved, poor old creature—
fairly clemmed, as they say in the North; here
we are at your place, Miss Garston. How
bright and inviting your parlour looks! I
wonder if I may ask to come in for a few
minutes, while I tell you about the other
case?'

Of course I could not do less than invite
him to enter after that; but I am afraid my
manner lacked enthusiasm, and betrayed the
fact that I was unwilling to entertain Mr.
Hamilton as a guest, for when I saw his face
in the lamp-light, he was regarding me with
some amusement.

'Cunliffe has done me no end of mischief,'
he said, as he offered to relieve me of my
wraps; 'that unfortunate speech has strongly
prejudiced you against me. Confess now, you
think me a very disagreeable person, because I
happened to disagree with you that evening.'

'Certainly not on that account,' I returned,
falling into the trap; and then we both laughed,
for I had as good as owned that I thought him
disagreeable. That laugh made us better friends.
I felt I no longer disliked him : it was certainly
not his fault that Providence had given him
that type of face, and I supposed one could get
used to it.

'I was in an evil mood that afternoon,' he
went on, and then I knew instinctively that he
wanted to efface his satirical words from my
memory. 'Things had gone wrong somehow—
for this world of ours is a mighty muddle

sometimes,' and here he gave an impatient sigh.
'It is a relief to human nature to vent one's
spleen on the first handy person that crosses
one's path, and, pardon me for saying so, you
were just a little aggressive yourself,' looking
at me rather dubiously as though he were not
quite sure how I should take this hit. My conscience told me that I had been far from peace-
able—on the contrary, I had been decidedly
cross—not that I would confess that this was
the case, so I only returned mildly that I
considered that he had been hard on me that
day, and had handled my pet theory very
roughly.

'Come, now you are talking like a reasonable woman, and I will plead guilty to some
severity. Let me own that I distrusted you,
Miss Garston. I have a horror of gush, and
what I call the working mania of young ladies,
and you had not proved to me then that you
could work. At the present day, if a girl is
restless and bad-tempered and cannot get on
with her own people, she takes up hospital-
nursing, and a rare muddle she makes of it
sometimes. I own hospital work is better than
the convent of the Middle Ages, where the

troublesome young ladies were safely immured; but, as I said before, I distrust the hysterical restlessness of the age.'

'No doubt you have a fair amount of argument on your side,' I replied, so meekly, that he looked at me, and then got up from his chair and said hastily that I was tired, and he was thoughtless to keep me waiting for my tea.

'Let me give you some, while you tell me about the case.' was my hospitable reply; for though I felt no special desire to prolong our tête-à-tête, mere civility prompted my offer.

He hesitated, then to my surprise sat down again, and said he would be very much obliged if I would give him a cup of tea, as he was tired too, and had to go farther and keep his dinner waiting.

I went out of the room to remove my hat and speak to Mrs. Barton. When I came back he was standing before Charlie's photograph and evidently studying it with some attention, but he made no remark about it; and I told him of my own accord that it was the portrait of my twin brother who had died two years ago.

'Indeed! There is no likeness; at least I

should not have known it was your brother.
This is often the case between relations,' he
continued hastily, as though he feared he had
hurt me. 'What a snug little berth you have,
Miss Garston, and everything so ship-shape
too. I suppose that is your piano, but I am
afraid you will have little time to practise,' and
then, as I handed him his tea, he threw himself
down in the easy-chair and seemed prepared
to enjoy himself.

Looking at Mr. Hamilton this evening I
could have believed he had two sides to his
character : he presented such a complete contrast to the Mr. Hamilton in Uncle Max's
study that I was quite puzzled by it. He had
certainly a clever face, and his smile was quick
and bright ; it was only in rest that his mouth
looked so stern and hard. I found myself
wondering once or twice if he had known any
great trouble that had embittered him.

'Well, I must tell you about poor Phebe
Locke,' he began suddenly. 'I want you to
find out what you can do for her. The Lockes
are respectable people : Phebe and her sister
were dressmakers. They live a little lower
down—at Woodbine Cottage.

'Some years ago spinal disease came on, and now Phebe is bed-ridden. She suffers a good deal at times, but her worst trouble is that her nerves are disordered, most likely from the dulness and monotony of her life. She suffers cruelly from low spirits, and no wonder, lying all day in that dull little back room. Her sister cannot sit with her, as Phebe cannot bear the noise of the sewing-machine, and the sight of the outer world seems to irritate her. The neighbours would come in to cheer her up, but she does not seem able to bear their loud voices. It is wonderful,' he continued musingly, 'how education and refinement train the voice; strange to say, though my voice is not particularly low, and certainly not sweet, it never seems to jar upon her.'

'Very likely not,' I returned quickly; 'no doubt she depends upon you for all her comforts; to most invalids the doctor's visit is the one bright spot in the day.'

'It seems strange that we do not project our own shadows sometimes and make our patient shiver,' he said with a touch of gruffness. 'It is little that I can do for Phebe, except order her a blister or ice when she needs it. One cannot touch the real nervous suffering : there is where I look to you for help ; a little cheerful talk now and then may lighten her burthen. Anyhow it would be a help for poor Miss Locke, who has a sad time of it trying to earn food for them both. There is a little niece who lives with them, a subdued uncanny little creature, who looks as though the childhood were crushed out of her ; you might take her in hand too.'

'I wonder if Phebe would like me to sing to her,' I observed quietly. 'I have found it answer sometimes in nervous illnesses.'

I thought my remark surprised him.

'It is a good idea,' he said slowly, 'you might try it. Of course it would depend a great deal on the quality of voice and style of singing. I wonder if you would allow me to judge of this'—looking meaningly at the piano ; but I shook my head at this and he did not press the point.

We had very little talk after this, for he went away almost directly—first arranging to meet me at Mrs. Marshall's about four the next day and go with me to Woodbine Cottage.

'You will find plenty of work, Miss Garston,' were his final words, 'so do not waste your strength unnecessarily;' and then he left the room, but came back a moment afterwards to say that his sisters meant to call on me, only they thought I was hardly settled yet; 'we must get Mr. Cunliffe to bring you up to Gladwyn—we must not let you mope.'

I thought there was little chance of this with Uncle Max and Mr. Tudor always looking after me. Mr. Hamilton had hardly closed the door before Uncle Max opened it again.

'So the enemy has tasted bread and salt, Ursula,' he said, looking excessively pleased; 'that is right, my dear—do not give way to absurd prejudices. You and Hamilton will get on splendidly by-and-by, when you get used to his brusque manner;' and though I did not quite endorse this opinion, I was obliged to acknowledge to myself that the last half-hour had not been so unpleasant after all.

CHAPTER X.

A DIFFICULT PATIENT.

I HAD a little talk with Granny the next
day.

Mrs. Marshall was dosing uneasily,
and I was sitting by Granny nursing the baby,
and waiting for Mr. Hamilton, when I felt her
cold wrinkled hand laid on mine.

'What is it, Elspeth?' I asked, thinking
she wanted something.

'What put it in your head, my bairn, to do
the Lord's work, that is what I am wanting to
know. I have been listening to you this morning singing like a bird about the house, with
all the bit creatures chirping about you, and
I said to myself, What could have put it into
her head to leave all her fine friends, and come
and wait on the likes of us old and sick folk
and young bairns?'

I do not know what there was in this speech that made me cry, but I know I had some difficulty in answering, but I told her a little about Charlie, and how sad I was, and how I loved the work, and she patted my hand softly all the time.

'Never fret, my bairn. You will not be lonely long, the Lord will see to that. He would not let you work for Him, and do nothing for you in return. Nay, that is not His way. Look at me—as Doctor said the other day, I have dree'd my weird; few and evil have been my days, like Jacob, but here I sit like a lady by the fire, warm and comfortable and hearty, thank God; and Andrew's wife lies on her death-bed, poor woman.'

'Yes; but, Elspeth, you sit there in the dark.'

'Eh, but it is peaceful and quiet-like, and the Lord bides with me, "and darkness and light are both alike to Him,"' finished Elspeth, reverently. And then I heard the click of the gate, and rose hastily, only the baby cried as I laid her on Elspeth's lap, and I had to stay a moment to pacify her.

Mr. Hamilton came in and stood by us.

'Do not hurry yourself, I can easily wait a few minutes if you are not ready; are you sure you are not too tired to come?' he continued, looking at me a little inquisitively, and I was certain that he noticed the trace of tears on my face. Why was it I never could speak of my darling quite calmly?

'I am perfectly ready, and baby has left off crying,' I returned, taking up my basket, and then we left the house together.

'I hope you do not suffer from low spirits like the rest of us,' he said in rather a kind tone, as we walked on. 'It is to be expected that a cross-grained fellow like myself should have fits of the blues occasionally; that is one thing I particularly admire about Cunliffe— however worried he is one never sees him out of humour; his ups and downs are never perceptible. I do believe he is less selfish than other people.'

'There is no one like Uncle Max,' I rejoined fervently.

'Is it not odd that we should suit each other so well?' he asked presently, 'for we are complete contrasts. I can bear him to say things to me that I would knock any other fellow down for saying. That is why I let him preach to me, because he honestly believes what he says and tries to act up to his profession.' He broke off here, for by this time we had reached Woodbine Cottage, and he unlatched the gate for me.

A thin-faced child with a cropped head and clean white pinafore opened the door, and dropped an alarmed curtsey when she saw us.

'Please, sir, Aunt Susan is out, and Aunt Phebe is very bad this afternoon, and cannot see any one. She is lying in the dark, and I was to let none of the neighbours in while Aunt Susan was away.'

'All right, Kitty, but Aunt Phebe will see me,' and he walked into the passage, and told the child to close the door gently. The room we passed was strewn with work material, and looked cold and comfortless, but a small kitchen opposite had a warm cozy aspect. Mr. Hamilton passed both rooms and tapped at a door lower down the passage, and then without waiting for an answer entered, and beckoned me to follow him.

A dark curtain had been drawn across the window, and the dim glow of a cindery fire scarcely gave sufficient light to discern the different pieces of furniture. Mr. Hamilton gave vent to a suppressed exclamation of impatience as he seized the poker, but I could not but notice the skilful and almost noiseless manner in which he manipulated the coals. Then he looked round for a match, and lighted a candle on the mantelpiece, in spite of a peevish remonstrance from the patient.

'You will make my head worse, doctor—nothing but the dark eases it.'

'Nonsense, Phebe, I know better than that,' he returned cheerfully, and then he stepped up to the bed—and I followed him. The woman who lay there was still young in years. She could not have been more than three or four and thirty, but every semblance of youth was crushed out of her by some subtle and mysterious suffering; it might have been the face of a dead woman only for the living eyes that locked at us.

The hopeless wistful look in those eyes gave me a singular shock. I had never seen human eyes with the same expression—they seemed as though they were appealing against some awful destiny. Once when I and Charlie were staying at Rutherford a beautiful spaniel belonging to Lesbia had been accidentally shot, while straying in some wood. The poor animal had dragged himself with pain and difficulty to the garden-gate, and there we found him. I shall never forget the wistfulness of the poor creature's eyes when his mistress knelt down and caressed him. He died a few minutes afterwards licking her hand. I could not help thinking of Tito when I first saw Phebe Locke; for the same unreasoning anguish seemed in the sick woman's eyes. A tormented soul looked out of them.

There was something rigid and uncompromising in the whole aspect of the sick room; there was nothing to tone down and soften the harsh details of bodily suffering; everything was in spotless order; the sheets were white as the driven snow; a formidable phalanx of medicine bottles stood on the small square table; there were no books, no pictures, no flowers: a sampler hung over the mantelpiece, that was all. I saw Mr. Hamilton glance disapprovingly at the row of bottles.

'I told Kitty to clear all that rubbish away,' he said curtly. 'Why do you not have something pleasanter to look at, Phebe?—some flowers or a canary ; you would find plenty of amusement in watching a canary.'

'Birds are never still for a moment; they would drive me mad,' returned Phebe, in the hollow tones that seemed natural to her; 'flowers are better, but what have I to do with flowers? Doctor,' her voice rising into a shrill crescendo, 'you must give me something to send me to sleep, or I shall go mad. I think, think, think, until my head is in a craze with pain and misery.'

'Well, well, we will see about it,' humouring her as though she were a child. 'Will you not speak to this lady, Phebe? She has come down here to help us all—sick people and unhappy people, and every one that wants help.'

'She can't do anything for me,' muttered Phebe, restlessly; 'no one—not even you, Doctor —can do anything for me. I am doomed— doomed before my time.'

Mr. Hamilton looked at me meaningly, as though to say, 'Now you see what you have to do ; this is more your work than mine.' I obeyed the hint and accosted the sick woman as cheerfully as though her dismal speech had not curdled my blood.

'I hope I shall be some comfort to you; it is hard indeed if no one can help you when you have so much to bear.'

'To bear!' repeating my words as though they stung her. 'I have laid here for three years—three years come Christmas Eve, Doctor —between these four walls: summer and winter, winter and summer, and never knew except by heat or cold what season of the year it was. And I am young—just turned four and thirty—and I may lay here thirty years more, unless I die or go mad.'

'Now, Phebe,' remonstrated Mr. Hamilton, and how gently he spoke, 'have I not told you over and over that things may mend yet if you will only be patient and good? You are just making things worse by bearing them so badly. Why, a friend of mine has been seven years on her back like you, and she is the happiest, cheeriest body; it is quite a pleasure to go into her room.'

'Maybe she is good and I am wicked,' returned Phebe, sullenly. 'I cannot help it, Doctor; it is one of my bad days, and nothing but wicked words come uppermost. The devil has a deal of power when a woman is chained as I am.'

'Don't you think you could exorcise the demon by a song, Miss Garston,' observed Mr. Hamilton, in an undertone. 'This is just the case where music may be a soothing influence; something must be tried for the poor creature.'

The proposition almost took away my breath. Sing now! before Mr. Hamilton! and yet how in sheer humanity could I refuse. I had often sung before to my patients, and had never minded it in the least; but before Mr. Hamilton!

'You need not think of me,' he continued provokingly—for of course I was thinking of him—'I am no critic in the musical line. Just try how it answers, will you,' and he walked away and turned his back to us, and seemed absorbed in the sampler.

For one minute I hesitated, and then I cleared my throat. 'I am going to sing something, Phebe. Mr. Hamilton thinks it will do you good,' and then, fearful lest her waywardness should stop me, I commenced at once with the first line of the beautiful hymn, 'Art thou weary, art thou languid?'

My voice trembled sadly at first, and my

burning face and cold hands testified to my nervousness; but after the first verse I forget Mr. Hamilton's presence and only remembered it was Charlie's favourite hymn I was singing, and sang it with a full heart.

When I had finished I bent over Phebe and asked if I should sing any more, and to my great delight she nodded assent. I sang 'Abide with me' and several other suitable hymns, and I did not stop until the hard look of woe in Phebe's eyes had softened into a more gentle expression.

As I paused I looked across the room. Mr. Hamilton was still standing by the mantelpiece perfectly motionless. He had covered his eyes with his hand, and seemed lost in profound thought. He absolutely started when I addressed him.

'Yes, we will go if you have finished,' but he did not look at me as he spoke. 'Phebe, has the young lady done you any good? Did you close your eyes and think you heard an angel singing? Now you must let me take her away, for she is very tired, and has worked hard to-day. To-morrow, if you ask her, she will come again.'

' I shall not wait to be asked,' I returned, answering the dumb, wistful look that greeted the doctor's words. ' Oh, yes, I shall come again to-morrow, and we will have a little talk, and I will bring you some flowers, and if you care to hear me sing I have plenty of pretty songs ; ' and then I kissed her forehead, for I felt strongly drawn to the poor creature, as though she were a strange, suffering sister, and I thought that the kiss and the song and the flowers would be a threefold cord of sympathy for her to bind round her harassed soul through the long hours of the night.

Mr. Hamilton followed me silently out, and on the threshold we encountered Susan Locke. She was a thin, subdued-looking woman, dressed in rusty black, with a careworn, depressed expression that changed into pleasure at the sight of Mr. Hamilton.

' Oh, Doctor, this is good of you, surely— and you so busy; it is one of Phebe's bad days, when nothing pleases her and she will have naught to say to us, but groan and groan until one's heart is pretty nigh broken. I was half hoping that you would look in on us and give her a bit of a word.'

O

'Miss Garston has done more than that,' replied Mr. Hamilton. 'I think you will find your sister a little cheered; give her something comfortable to eat and drink, and speak as cheerfully as you can. Good night, Miss Locke;' and then he motioned to me to precede him down the little garden. Mr. Hamilton was so very silent all the way home that I was somewhat puzzled; he did not speak at all about Phebe—only said that he was afraid that I was very tired, and that he was the same; and when we came in sight of the cottage, he left me rather abruptly—if it had not been for his few approving words to Susan Locke, I should have thought something had displeased him.

Uncle Max made me feel a little uncomfortable the next morning. I met him as I was starting for my daily work, and he walked with me to Mrs. Marshall's.

'I was up at Gladwyn last evening, Ursula,' he began. 'Miss Elizabeth is still away, but the other ladies asked very kindly after you. Miss Hamilton means to call on you one afternoon, only she seems puzzled to know how she is ever to find you at home. I cannot think

what put Hamilton into such a bad temper ; he
scarcely spoke to any of us, and looked horribly
cranky, only I laughed at him and he got
better ; he never mentioned your name ; you
have not fallen out again, eh—little she-bear? '
looking at me rather anxiously.

'Oh dear no ; we are perfectly civil to
each other ; I understand him better now.' But
all the same, I could not help wondering as I
parted from Max what could have made Mr.
Hamilton so strangely silent.

It was still early in the afternoon when I
found myself free to go and see Phebe ; she
had been on my mind all day, and had kept
me awake for a long time ; those miserable
eyes haunted me. I longed so to comfort her.
Miss Locke opened the door ; I thought she
seemed pleased to see me, but she eyed my
basket of flowers dubiously.

'Phebe is looking for you, Miss Garston,
though she says nothing about it—it is not her
way ; but I see her eyes turning to the door
every now and then, and she made Kitty open
the curtains ; if I may make so bold, those
flowers are not for Phebe, surely?'

'Yes, indeed they are, Miss Locke. Dr.

Hamilton wishes her to have something pleasant to look at.' But Miss Locke only shook her head.

'The neighbours have sent in flowers often and often, and she has made me carry them out of the room ; the Vicar used to send them, too, but he knows now that it is no manner of use—she always says they do not put flowers in tombs, only outside them ; she will have it she is living in a tomb.'

'We must get this idea out of her head,' I returned cheerfully, for I was obstinately bent on having my own way about the flowers.

Kitty was sewing on a little stool by the window ; the curtains were undrawn, so that the room was tolerably light, and might have been cheerful, only an ugly wire blind shut out all view of the little garden.

I could not help marvelling at the strange perversity that could wilfully exclude every possible alleviation ; there must be some sad warp or twist of the mental nature that could be so prolific of unwholesome fancies. As I turned to the bed I thought Phebe looked even more ghastly in the daylight than she had done last evening ; her skin was yellow and shrivelled, like the skin of an old woman ; her

eyes looked deep set and gloomy, but their
expression struck me as more human ; her
thin lips even wore the semblance of a smile.

When I had greeted her, and had drawn
from her rather reluctantly that she had had
some hours' sleep the previous night, I spoke
to Kitty. The little creature looked so subdued
and moped in the miserable atmosphere, that I
was full of pity for her, so I showed her a new
skipping-rope that I had bought on my way,
and bade her ask her Aunt Susan's permission
to go out and play.

The child's dull eyes brightened in a
moment—'May I go out, Aunt Phebe?' she
asked breathlessly.

'Yes, go, if you like,' was the somewhat
ungracious answer. 'She is glad enough to get
away from me,' she muttered, when Kitty had
shut the door gently behind her. 'Children
have no heart; she is an ungrateful, selfish
little thing ; but they are all that—we clothe
her and feed her, and it is little we get out of
her in return ; and Susan is working her fingers
to the bone for the two of us.'

I took no notice of this outburst, and commenced clearing away the medicine-bottles to

make room for my basket of chrysanthemums and ivy-leaves. Uncle Max had procured them for me, but I had no idea as I arranged them that they had come from Gladwyn.

Phebe watched my movements very gloomily; she evidently disapproved of the whole proceeding. I carried out the bottles to Miss Locke, and begged her to throw them away—'they are of no use to her,' I observed. 'Mr. Hamilton intends to send her a new mixture, and this array of half-emptied phials is simply absurd—it is just a whim. If your sister asks for them when I have gone, you can tell her that Miss Garston ordered them to be destroyed.'

On my return to the room I found Phebe lying with her eyes closed. I could have laughed outright at her perversity, for of course she had shut them to exclude the sight of the flower-basket, though it was the loveliest little bit of colour, the dark red chrysanthemum nestled so prettily amongst trails of tiny variegated ivy. I resolved to punish her for this piece of morbid obstinacy, and took down the wire blind; she was speechless with anger when she found out what I had done, but I was resolved not to humour these ridiculous fancies ; the dull wintry light was not too much for her.

'You must not be allowed to have your own way so entirely,' I said, laughing, 'your sister is very wrong to give in to you. Mr. Hamilton wishes your room to be more cheerful—he says the dull surroundings depress and keep you low and desponding, and I must carry out his orders, and try how we are to make your room a little brighter. Now,'—as she seemed about to speak—'I am going to sing to you, and then we will have a talk.'

'I don't care to hear singing to-day, my head buzzes so 'with all this flack,' was the sullen answer ; but I took no notice of this illtempered remark, and begun a little Scotch ballad that I thought was bright and spirited.

She closed her eyes again, with an expression of weariness and disgust, that made me smile in spite of my efforts to keep serious ; but I soon found out that she was listening, and so I sang one song after another, without pausing for any comment, and pretended not to notice when the haggard weary eyes unclosed, and fixed themselves first on the flowers, next on my face, and last and longest at the strip of lawn, with the bare gooseberry bushes and the narrow path edged with privet.

When I had sung several ballads, I waited for a minute and then commenced Bishop Ken's evening hymn, but my voice shook a little as I saw a sudden heaving under the bed-clothes, and in another moment the large slow tears coursed down Phebe's thin face. It was hard to finish the hymn, but I would not have dispensed with the Gloria.

'What is it, Phebe?' I asked gently, when I had finished. 'I am sorry that I have made you cry.'

'You need not be sorry,' she sobbed at last, with difficulty, 'it eases my head, and I thought nothing would ever draw a tear from me again. I was too miserable to cry, and they say—I have read it somewhere, in the days when I used to read—that there is no such thing as a tear in Hell.'

I tried not to look astonished at this strange speech. I must let this poor creature talk, or how should I ever find out the root of her disease; so I answered quietly that no doubt she was right, that in that place of outer darkness there should be weeping, without tears,

and a gnashing of teeth, beside which our
bitterest human sorrow would seem like
nothing.

'That is true,' she returned, with a groan ;
'but, Miss Garston, hell has begun for me here ;
for three years I have been in torment, and
rightly too—and rightly too—for I never was
a good woman, never like Susan, who read her
Bible and went to church—oh, she is a good
creature is Susan.'

'I am glad to hear it, Phebe ; so, you see,
your affliction, heavy as it is—and I am not
saying it is not heavy—is not without alleviation. The Merciful Father, who has laid this
cross upon you, has given you this kind companion as a consoler. What a comfort you must
be to each other, what a divine work has been
given to you both to do—to bring up that
motherless little creature, who must owe her
very life and happiness to you !'

She lay and looked at me with an expression
of bewildered astonishment, and at this moment
Miss Locke opened the door, carrying a little
tea-tray for her sister. I had a glimpse of
Kitty curled up on the mat outside the door,
with the skipping-rope still in her hand. She

had evidently been listening to the singing, for she crept away, but in the distance I could hear her humming 'Ye banks and braes' in a sweet childish treble that was very harmonious and true.

CHAPTER XI.

ONE OF GOD'S HEROINES.

O. I was quite right when I told poor Phebe that her sad case was not without alleviation. I was still more sure of the truth of my words when I saw with what care Miss Locke had prepared the invalid's meal, and how gently she helped to place her in a proper position. There was evidently no want of love between the sisters ; only on one side the love was more self-sacrificing and unselfish than on the other. It needed only a look at Susan Locke's spare form and thin, careworn face, to tell me that she was wearing herself out in her sister's service. Phebe looked in her face and broke into a harsh laugh, to poor Susan's great alarm.

'What do you think Miss Garston has been saying, Susan? That we must be a comfort to each other. Fancy my being a comfort to you! You poor thing, when I am the plague and burden of your life.' And she laughed again in a way that was scarcely mirthful.

'Nay, Phebe, you have no need to say such things,' returned her sister, sadly ; but she was probably used to these sort of speeches. 'I am bound to take care of you and Kitty, who are all I have left in the world. It is not that I find it hard, but that you might make it easier by looking a little cheered sometimes.'

Phebe took this gentle rebuke somewhat scornfully.

'Cheered! The woman actually says cheered, when I am already on the borderland of the place of torment. Was I not as good as dead and buried three years ago? And did not father always tell us that hell begins in this world for the wicked?'

'Ay, that was father's notion ; and I was never clever enough to argue with him. But you are not wicked, my woman, only a bit tiresome and perverse, and wanting in faith.' And Miss Locke, who was used to these wild

moods, patted her sister's shoulder, and bade
her drink her tea before it got cold, in a sensible
matter-of-fact way, that was not without its
influence on the wayward creature ; for she did
not refuse the comforting draught.

I took my leave soon after this after pro-
mising to repeat my visit on the next evening.
Phebe bade me good-bye rather coldly, but I
took no notice of her contrary mood. Miss
Locke followed me out of the room, and asked
me anxiously what I thought of her sister.

'It is difficult to judge,' I returned, hesitating a little. 'You must remember this is only
my second visit, and I have not made much way
with her. She is in a state of bodily and mental
discomfort very painful to witness. If I am not
mistaken, she is driving herself half crazy with
introspection and self-will. You must not give
way to this morbid desire to increase her own
wretchedness. She needs firmness as well as
kindness.'

Miss Locke looked at me wistfully a moment.

'What am I to do? She would fret herself
into a fever if I crossed her whims. Directly
you have left the house she will be asking for
that wire blind again, though it would do her

poor eyes good to see the thrushes feeding on the lawn, and there is the little robin that comes to us every winter and taps at the window for crumbs; but she would shut them all out—birds, and sunshine, and flowers.'

'Just as she would shut out her Father's love, if she could; but it is all round her, and no inward or outward darkness can hinder that. Miss Locke, you must be very firm. You must not move the flowers or replace the blind on any pretext whatever. She must be comforted in spite of herself. She reminds me of some passionate child who breaks all its toys because some wish has been denied. We are sorry for the child's disappointment, but a wise parent would inflict punishment for the fit of passion.'

Miss Locke sighed; her mouth twitched with repressed emotion. She was evidently an affectionate, reticent woman, who found it difficult to express her feelings.

'I am keeping you standing all this time,' she said apologetically, 'and I might have asked you to sit down a minute in our little kitchen. Let me pour you out a cup of tea, Miss Garston. Kitty and I were just going to begin.'

I accepted this offer, as I thought Miss Locke evidently wanted to speak to me. She seemed pleased at my acquiescence, and told Kitty to stay with her Aunt Phebe a few minutes.

'I have baked a nice hot cake with currants in it, Kitty,' she said persuasively, 'and you shall have your share, hot and buttered, if you will be patient and wait a little.'

'She is a good little thing,' I observed, as the child reluctantly withdrew to her dreary post, after a longing look at the table, while Miss Locke placed a rocking-chair with a faded green cushion by the fire, and opened the oven door to inspect the cake. 'It is dull work for the little creature to be so much in the sick room. It is hardly a wholesome atmosphere for a child.'

Miss Locke shook her head as though she endorsed this opinion.

'What am I to do?' she returned sorrowfully. 'Kitty is young, but she has to bear our burthens. I spare her all I can; but when I am at my dressmaking Phebe cannot be left alone, and she has learnt to be quiet and handy, and can do all sorts of things for Phebe. I know it is

not good for her living alone with us, but the
Lord has ordered the child's life as well as
ours,' she finished reverently.

'We must see what can be done for Kitty,'
was my answer. 'She can be free to play
while I am with your sister. I sent her out
with her new skipping-rope this evening. What
brought her back so soon?'

'It was the singing,' returned Miss Locke,
smiling. 'The street-door was just ajar, and
Kitty crept in and curled herself up on the mat.
It sounded so beautiful, you see; for Kitty
and I only hear singing at church, and it is
not often I can get there, with Phebe wanting
me; so it did us both good, you may be sure
of that.'

I could not but be pleased at this simple
tribute of praise, but something else struck me
more, the unobtrusive goodness and self-denial
of Susan Locke. What a life hers must be!
I hinted at this as gently as I could.

'Ay, Phebe has always been a care to me,'
she sighed. 'She was never as strong and hearty
as other girls, and she wanted her own way,
and fretted when she could not get it. Father
spoiled her, and mother gave into her more

than she did to me ; and when trouble came all
along of Robert Owen, and he used her cruel,
just flinging her aside when he saw some one he
fancied more than Phebe, and driving her mad
with spite and jealousy, then she let herself go,
as it were. She was never religious, not to
speak of all the time she kept company with
Robert, so when her hopes of him came to an
end she had nothing to support her—it needs
plenty of faith to make us bear our troubles
patiently.'

'And then her health failed.'

'Yes ; and mother died, and father followed
her within six months, and Phebe could not be
with them, and she took on about that ; she has
had a deal of trouble, and that is why I cannot
find it in my heart to be hard on her—-she was
that fond of Robert, though he was a worthless
sort of fellow, that, as the saying is, she worshipped the ground he walked on. Ah, Phebe
was bonnie-looking then, though she was never
over-strong, and had not much colour ; but he
need not have called her a sickly ill-tempered
wench when he threw her over and married
Nancy. It was a cruel way to serve a woman
that loved him as Phebe did'.

' She has certainly had her share of trouble. How long ago did this happen to your sister ? '

' It must be five years since Robert and Nancy were married. Phebe was never the same woman since then, though her health did not fail for a year or more afterwards ; Mr. Hamilton always says she has had a good riddance of Robert. He never thought much of him, and he has told me that it is far better that Phebe never had a chance of marrying him, for she would have been a sad burthen to any man—and she would not have had you to nurse her ; ' and Miss Locke's careworn face brightened. ' That is just what I tell myself, when I am out of heart about her ; the Lord knew Robert would have been a cruel husband to her—for he is not too kind to Nancy—and so He kept Phebe away from him. Phebe is not one to bear unkindness —it just maddens her, and we have all spoilt her.'

' Just so, and she knows her power over you ; I am afraid she gives you a great deal to bear, Miss Locke.'

' I never mind it from her,' she answered simply. ' She is all I have in the world except

Kitty, and I am thinking what I can do for her from morning to night; that is the best and the worst of my work, one need never stop thinking for it. Sometimes, when I am tired, or things have gone wrong with my customers, or I am a bit behindhand with the rent, I wish I could talk it over with her—it would ease me somehow; but I never do give way to the feeling, for it would only fret and worry her.'

'You are wrong,' I returned warmly. 'Mr. Hamilton would tell you so if you asked him; any worry, any outside trouble, would be better for Phebe than this unhealthy feeding on herself. Take my advice, Miss Locke—talk about yourself and your own troubles, Phebe is fond of you, it will rouse her to enter more into your life.'

Miss Locke shook her head, and the tears came into her mild hazel eyes.

'There is One who knows it all. I'll not be troubling my poor Phebe,' she said, and her hands trembled a little. Kitty came in at this moment and said her Aunt Phebe wanted her, so we were obliged to break off the conversation.

I thought about it all rather sadly as I sat

by my solitary fire that evening with Tinker's
head on my lap.   He had taken to me, and I
always found him waiting for my return ; but it
was less of Phebe than of Susan I was thinking.
I was so absorbed in my reflections that Uncle
Max's voice outside quite startled me.

'May I come in, Ursula ?' he said, thrusting
in his head.   'I have been at the choir practice,
so I thought I would call as I passed.'

Of course I gave him a warm welcome, and
he drew his chair to the opposite side of the
fire, and declared he felt very comfortable ;
then he asked me why I was looking grave,
and if I were tired of my solitude.   I disclaimed
this indignantly, and gave him a sketch of my
day's work, ending with my talk to Susan Locke.'

He seemed interested, and listened attentively.

'It is such a sad case, Max—poor Phebe's,
I mean—but I am almost as sorry for her sister.
Susan Locke is such a good woman.'

'You would say so if you knew all, Ursula,
but Miss Locke would never tell you herself.
When Phebe's illness came on, and Hamilton
told them that she might not get well for a
year, or two, or perhaps longer, Susan broke off

her own engagement to stay with her sister. Her father was just dead, and the child Kitty had to live with them.'

' Miss Locke engaged!' I exclaimed in some surprise, for it had never struck me that the homely middle-aged woman had this sort of experience in her life.

Max looked amused.

' In that class they do not always choose youth and beauty. Certainly Susan Locke was neither young nor handsome, but she was a neat-looking body, only she has aged of late. Do you want to know all about it? Well, she was engaged to a man named Duncan—he was a widower with three or four children ; he had the all-sort shop down the village, only he moved last year. He was a respectable man and had a comfortable little business, and I dare say he thought Miss Locke would make a good mother to his children. She told me all about it, poor thing ! She would have liked to marry Duncan ; she was fond of him, and thought he would have made her a steady husband ; but with Phebe on her hands she could not do her duty to him or the children.

'"And there is Kitty—and he has enough of his own; and a sickly body like Phebe would hinder the comfort of the house, and I have promised mother to take care of her." And then she asked my opinion. Well, I could not but own that with the shop and the house to mind, and five children, counting Kitty, and a bed-ridden invalid, her hands would be over-weighted with work and worry.

'"I think so too," she answered as quietly as possible, "and I have no right to burthen Duncan. I am sure he will listen to reason when I tell him Phebe is against our marrying." And she never said another word about it. But Duncan came to me about six months afterwards and asked me to put up his banns.

'"I wanted Susan Locke," he said, in a shamefaced manner, "but that sister of hers hinders our marrying; so, as I must think of the children, I have got Janet Sharpe to promise me. She is a good, steady lass, and Susan speaks well of her."'

Uncle Max had told his story without interruption. I listened to it with almost painful interest.

With what quiet self-denial this homely

woman had put aside her own hopes of happiness for the sake of the sickly creature dependent on her ! She had owned her affection for Duncan with the utmost simplicity ; but in her unselfishness she refused to burthen him with her responsibilities. If she married him she must do her duty by him and his children, and she felt that Phebe would be a drag on her strength and time.

'She is a good woman, Uncle Max,' I observed when he had finished. 'She is working herself to death, and Phebe never gives her a word of comfort.'

'How can you expect it?' he replied quietly. 'You cannot draw comfort out of empty wells, and poor Phebe's heart is like a broken cistern, holding nothing.'

'But surely you talk to her, Uncle Max?'

'I have tried to do so,' he answered sadly ; 'but for the last year she has refused to see me, and Hamilton has advised me to keep away. If I cross the threshold it is to see Miss Locke. I thought it was a whim at first, and I sent Tudor in my stead ; but she was so rude to him, and lashed herself into such a fury against us clerics, that he came back looking quite scared, and asked why I had sent him to a mad woman.'

'She was angry with me to-day.' And I told him about the blind.

'That is right, Ursula,' he said encouragingly. 'You have made a good beginning; the singing may do more to soften her strange nature than all our preaching. You will be a comfort to Miss Locke, at any rate.' And then he stopped, and looked at me rather wistfully, as though he longed to tell me something but could not make up his mind to do it. 'You will be a comfort to us all if you go on in this way,' he continued; and then he surprised me by asking if I had not yet seen the ladies from Gladwyn.

The question struck me as rather irrelevant, but I took care not to say so as I answered in the negative.

'You have been here nearly a week; they might have risked a call by this time,' he returned, knitting his brows as though something perplexed him; but I broke in on his reflections rather impatiently.

'I declare, Max, you have quite piqued my curiosity about these people; some mystery seems to attach to Gladwyn. I shall expect to see something very wonderful.'

'Then you will be disappointed,' he returned quietly, not a bit offended by my petulance. 'I cannot help wishing you to make acquaintance with them, as they are such intimate friends of mine, and I think it will be a mutual benefit.'

Then, as I made no reply to this, he went on, still more mildly :

'I confess I should like your opinion of them. I have a great reliance in your intuition and common sense ; and you are so deliciously frank and outspoken, Ursula, that I shall soon know what you think. Well, I must not stay gossiping here. Your company is very charming, my dear, but I have letters to write before bedtime. You will see our friends in church on Sunday. I hear Miss Elizabeth comes home to-morrow ; she is the lively one—not quite of the merry Pecksniff order, but still a bright, chatty little lady.

> From morning till night
> It is Betty's delight
> To chatter and talk without stopping.

You know the rest, Ursula, my dear. By the

bye,' opening the door, and looking cautiously into the passage, ' I wonder whom the Bartons are entertaining in the kitchen to-night ?   I hear a masculine voice.'

' It is only Mr. Hamilton,' I returned indifferently. ' I heard him come in half an hour ago ; he is giving Nathaniel a lesson in mathematics.'

' To be sure.   What a good fellow he is ! ' in an enthusiastic tone. ' Well, good-night, child ; do not sit up late,' and he vanished.

I am afraid I disregarded this injunction, for I wanted to write to my poor Jill—who was never absent from my mind—and Lesbia ; and I was loth to leave the fireside, and too much excited for sleep.

When I had finished my letters I still sat on gazing into the bright caverns of coal, and thinking over Susan Locke's history.

' How many good people there are in the world ! ' I said half aloud ; but I almost jumped out of my chair at the sound of a deep, angry voice on the other side of the door.

' It is a thriftless, wasteful sort of thing burning the candle at both ends. Women have very little common sense after all.'

I extinguished the lamp hastily, for of course Mr. Hamilton's growl was meant for me, though it was addressed to Nathaniel. I heard him close the door a moment afterwards, and Nathaniel crept back into the kitchen. I woke rather tired the next day and owned he was right, for I found my duties somewhat irksome that morning. The feeling did not pass off, and I actually discovered that I was dreading my visit to Phebe, only of course I scouted it as nonsense.

Miss Locke was out, and Kitty opened the door. Her little demure face brightened when she saw me, and especially when I placed a large brown-paper parcel in her arms, of that oblong shape dear to all doll-loving children, and bade her take it into the kitchen.

'It is too dark and cold for you to play outside, Kitty,' I observed, 'so perhaps you will make the acquaintance of the blue-eyed baby I have brought you; when Aunt Susan comes in, you can ask her for some pieces to dress her in, for her paper robe is rather cold.'

Kitty's eyes grew wide with surprise and delight as she ran off with her treasure; the baby-doll would be a playmate for the

lonely child, and solace those weary hours in
the sick room.   I would rather have brought
her a kitten, but I felt instinctively that no
animal would be tolerated by the invalid.

It was somewhat dark when I entered the
room, but one glance showed me that my
directions had been obeyed ; the window was
unshaded and the flowers were in their place.

Phebe was lying watching the fire.   I saw
at once that she was in a better mood.   The
few questions I put to her were answered
quietly and to the point, and there was no
excitement or exaggeration in her manner.

I did not talk much.   After a minute or
two I sat down by the uncurtained window
and began to sing as usual.   I commenced
with a simple ballad, but very soon my songs
merged into hymns.   It began to be a pleasure
to me to sing in that room.   I had a strange
feeling as though my voice were keeping the
evil spirits away.   I thought of the shepherd
boy who played before Saul and refreshed the
king's tormented mind ; and now and then
an unuttered prayer would rise to my lips that
in this way I might be able to comfort the sad
soul that truly Satan had bound.

When my voice grew a little weary, I rose softly and took down the old brown sampler, as I wished to replace it by a little picture I had brought with me.

It was a sacred photograph of the crucifixion, in a simple Oxford frame, and had always been a great favourite with me; it was less painful in its details than other delineations of this subject—the face of the Divine sufferer wore an expression of tender pity. Beneath the cross the Blessed Virgin and St. John stood with clasped hands—adopted love and most sacred responsibility—receiving sanction and benediction.

I had scarcely hung it on the nail before Phebe's querulous voice remonstrated with me.

'Why can you not leave well alone, Miss Garston? I was thanking you in my heart for the music, but you have just driven it away. I cannot have that picture before my eyes; it is too painful.'

'You will not find it so,' I replied quietly; 'it is a little present I have brought you. My dead brother bought it for me when he was a boy at school, and it is one of the things I most prize. He is dead, you

know, and that makes it doubly dear to me.
That is why I want you to have it, because I
have so much and you so little.'

My speech moved her a little, for her great
eyes softened as she looked at me.

'So you have been in trouble, too,' she
said softly. 'And yet you can sing like a bird
that has lost its way and finds itself nearly at
the gate of Paradise.'

'Shall I tell you about my trouble?' I returned, sitting down by the bed. It wrung
my heart to talk of Charlie, but I knew the
history of his suffering and patience would
teach Phebe a valuable lesson.

An hour passed by unheeded, and when I
had finished I exclaimed at the lateness of the
hour.

'Ay, you have tired yourself—you look
quite pale,' was her answer; 'but you have
made me forget myself for the first time in my
life.' She stopped, and then with more effort
continued, 'Come again to-morrow, and I will
tell you my trouble; it is worse than yours,
and has made me the crazy creature you see.
Yes, I will tell you all about it;' but half
crying, as though she had little hope of con-

testing my will, 'You will not leave that picture to make my heart ache more than it does now ? '

'My poor Phebe,' I said, kissing her, ' when your heart once aches for the thought of another's sorrow your healing will have begun. Let that picture say to you what no one has said to you before, " that all your life you have been an idolater, that you have worshipped only yourself and one other—— " '

'Whom ?   What do you mean ?   Have you heard of Robert ? ' she asked excitedly.

' To-morrow is Sunday,' I returned, touching her softly.   ' I am going to church in the morning, and I shall not be here until evening ; but we shall have time then for a long talk, and you shall tell me everything ; ' and then without waiting for an answer I left the room. It was late indeed.   Miss Locke had long returned, and was busying herself over her sister's supper ; she held up her finger to me smiling as I passed, and I peeped in.

Kitty was lying on the rug fast asleep with the doll in her arms.

' I found them like this when I came in,' whispered Miss Locke ; ' she must have been listening to the music and fallen asleep. How late you have stopped with Phebe; it is nearly eight o'clock!'

'I do not think the time has been wasted,' I answered cheerfully, as I bade her good-night and stepped out into the darkness. Is time ever wasted, I wonder, when we stop in our daily work to give one of these weak ones a cup of cold water? It is not for me to answer, only our recording angel knows how some such little deed of kindness may brighten some dim struggling life that seems over-full of pain.

CHAPTER XII.

A MISSED VOCATION.

T was pleasant to wake to bright sunshine the next morning, and to hear the sparrows twittering in the ivy.

It had been my intention to set apart Sunday as much as possible as a day of rest and refreshment. Of course I could not expect always to control the various appeals for my help or to be free from my patients, but by management I hoped to secure the greater part of the day for myself.

I had told Peggy not to expect me at the cottage until the afternoon; everything was in such order that there was no necessity for me to forego the morning service. My promise to Phebe Locke would keep me a prisoner for the evening, but I determined that her sister and Kitty should be set free to go to church, so my loss would be their gain.

I thought of Jill as I dressed myself. She had often owned to me that the Sundays at Hyde Park Gate were not to her taste. Visitors thronged the house in the afternoon; Sara discussed her week's amusements with her friends or yawned over a novel; the morning's sermon was followed as a matter of course by a gay luncheon party. 'What does it mean, Ursula? Jill would say, opening her big black eyes as widely as possible; 'I do not understand. Mr. Erskine has been telling us that we ought to renounce the world and our own wills, and not to follow the multitude to do foolishness, and all the afternoon mother and Sara have been talking about dresses for the fancy-ball; is there one religion for church and another for home? Do we fold it up and put it away with our prayer-books in the little book-cupboard that father locks so carefully?' finished Jill, with girlish scorn.

Poor Jill, she had a wide generous nature, with great capabilities, but she was growing up in a chilling atmosphere. Young girls are terribly honest; they dig down to the very root of things; they drag off the swathing cloths from the mummy face of conventionality. What does it mean? they ask. Is there truth any-where? Endless shams surround them; people listen to sermons, then they shake off the dust of the holy place carefully from the very hem of their garments; their religion, as Jill expressed, is left beside their prayer-books. Ah! if one could but see clearly, with eyes purged from every remnant of earthliness—see as the angels do—the thick fog of unrisen and unprayed prayers clinging to the rafters of every empty church, we might well shudder in the clogging heavy atmosphere.

Jill had not more religion than many other girls, but she wanted to be true; the incon-sistency of human nature baffled and perplexed her; she was not more ready to renounce the world than Sara was, but she wished to know the inner meaning of things, and in this I longed to help her. I could not help thinking of her tenderly and pitifully as I walked down the road leading to the little Norman church. I was early, and the building was nearly empty when I entered the porch; but it was quiet and restful to sit there and review the past week, and watch the sunshine lighting up the red brick walls and touching the rood-screen, while a faint purple gleam fell on the chancel pavement.

Two ladies entered the seat before me, and I looked at them a little curiously.

They were both very handsomely dressed, but it was not their fashionable appearance that attracted me. I had caught sight of a most beautiful and striking face belonging to one of them that somehow riveted my attention.

The lady was apparently very young, and had a tall graceful figure, and strange colourless hair that looked as though it ought to have been golden, only the gloss had faded out of it, but it was lovely hair, fine and soft as a baby's.

As she rose she slightly turned round, and our eyes met for a moment; they were large melancholy eyes, and the face, beautiful as it was, was very worn and thin, and absolutely without colour. I could see her profile plainly all through the service, but the dull impassive expression of the countenance that she had turned upon me gave me a sensation of pain, she looked like a person who had experienced some great trouble or undergone some terrible illness. I could not make up my mind which it could be.

The other lady was much older, and had no claims to beauty. I could see her face plainly, for she looked round once or twice as though she were expecting some one.

She must have been over thirty, and had rather a singular face ; it was thin, dark-complexioned, and very sallow ; she was a stylish-looking woman, but her appearance did not interest me. To my surprise, just as the service commenced Mr. Hamilton came in and joined them. So these must be the ladies from Gladwyn, I thought. That beautiful pale girl must be his sister Gladys, and the other one Miss Darrell.

I tried to keep my attention to my own devotions, but every now and then my eyes would stray to the lovely face before me. Mr. Hamilton's behaviour was irreproachable. I could hear his voice following all the responses, and he sang the hymns very heartily.

I think he knew I was behind him, for he handed me a hymn-book, with a slight smile, when I was offering to share mine with a young woman. Miss Darrell gave me a curiously penetrating look when she came out that did not quite please me, but the girl who followed her did not seem to notice my presence. I sat still in my place for a minute, as I did not wish to encounter them in the porch. I had lingered so long that the congregation had quite dispersed when I got out, but, to my surprise, I could see the three walking very slowly down the road. Could they have been waiting for me? I wondered, but I dismissed this idea as absurd.

But I could not forget the face that had so interested me—and when I encountered Uncle Max on his way to the children's service I questioned him at once about the two ladies.

'Yes, you are right, Ursula,' he said, a little absently. 'The one with fair hair was Miss Gladys; her cousin, Miss Darrell, sat by Hamilton.'

'But you never told me how beautiful she was,' I replied, in rather an injured voice. 'She has a perfect face, only it is so worn and unhappy-looking.'

'You must not keep me,' observed Max, hurriedly, 'Miss Darrell wants to speak to me before service.' And he rushed off, leaving me standing in the middle of the path rather wondering at his abruptness, for the bell had not commenced.

A little farther on, I came face to face with Miss Darrell; she was walking with Mr. Tudor, and seemed talking to him with much animation.

She bowed slightly, as he took off his hat to me, in a graceful well-bred manner, but her face prepossessed me even less than it had done in the morning. She had keen, dark eyes like Mr. Hamilton's, only they somehow repelled me. I was somewhat quick with my likes and dislikes, as I had proved by the dislike I had taken to Mr. Hamilton. This feeling was wearing off, and I was no longer so strongly prejudiced against him. I might even find Miss Darrell less repelling when I spoke to her. She was evidently a gentlewoman; her movements were quiet and graceful, and she had a good carriage.

I was somewhat surprised on reaching the cottage to find Mr. Hamilton sitting by my patient. He had Janie on his knee, and seemed as though he had been there for some time, but he rose at once when he saw me.

'I was waiting for you, Miss Garston,' he said quietly. 'I wanted to give you some directions about Mrs. Marshall,' and when he had finished, he said a little abruptly :

'What made you so long coming out of church this morning? I was waiting to introduce my sister and cousin to you, but you were determined to disappoint me.'

I was a little confused by this.

'Did you recognise me?' I asked rather tamely.

'No—not in that smart bonnet,' was the unexpected reply. 'I did not identify the wearer with the village nurse, until I heard your voice in the Te Deum—you can hardly disguise your voice, Miss Garston — my cousin Etta pricked up her ears when she heard it;' and then, as I made no answer, he picked up his hat with rather an amused air and wished me good-bye.

I was rather offended at the mention of my bonnet : the little grey wing that relieved its sombre black trimmings could hardly be called smart—a word I abhorred—but he probably said it to tease me.

'Ay, the doctor has been telling us you

have a voice like a skylark,' observed Elspeth;
'but I have been thinking it must be more like
an angel's voice, my bairn, since you mostly
use it to sing the Lord's praises, and to cheer
the sick folk round you—that is more than a
skylark does.'

So he had been praising my voice. What
an odd man!

I stayed at the cottage about two hours,
and read a little to the children and Elspeth,
and then I started for the Lockes.

Kitty clapped her hands when she heard
she was to go to church with her Aunt Susan.
I found out afterwards the child had always
gone alone.

Phebe was evidently expecting me, for her
eyes were fixed on the door as I entered, and
the same shadowy smile I had seen once before
swept over her wan features when she saw me.
She seemed ready and eager to talk, but I ad-
hered to my usual programme. I was rather
afraid that our conversation would excite her,
so I wanted to quiet her first. I sang a few of
my favourite hymns, and then read the evening
psalms. She heard me somewhat reluctantly,
but when I had finished her face cleared, and

without any preamble she commenced her story.

I never remember that recital without pain. It positively wrung my heart to listen to her. I had heard the outline of her sad story from her sister's lips, but it had lacked colour; it had been a simple statement of facts, and no more.

But now Phebe's passionate words seemed to clothe it with power; the very sight of the ghastly and almost distracted face on the pillow gave a miserable pathos to the story. It was in vain to check excitement while the unhappy creature poured out the history of her wrongs —the old, old story, of a credulous woman's heart being trampled upon and tortured by an unworthy lover, was enacted again before me.

'I just worshipped the ground he walked on, and he threw me aside like a broken toy,' she said over and over again. 'And the worst of it is that, villain as he is, I cannot unlove him, though I am that mad with him sometimes that I could almost murder him.'

'Love is strong as death, and jealousy is cruel as the grave,' I muttered, half to myself, but she overheard me.

' Ay, that is just true,' she returned eagerly,
' there are times when I hate Robert and Nancy
and would like to haunt them. Did I not tell
you, Miss Garston, that hell had begun with
me already? I was never a good woman—
never, not even when I was happy and Robert
loved me. I was just full of him, and wanted
nothing else in heaven and earth ; and when the
trouble came, and father and mother died, and
I lay here like a log—only a log has not got a
living heart in it—I seemed to go mad with the
anger and unhappiness, and I felt " the worm
that dieth not, and the fire that is not
quenched." '

I stooped over and wiped her poor lips and
poor head, for she was fearfully exhausted, and
then in a perfect passion of pity closed her face
between my hands, and bade God bless her.

' What do you mean ? ' she said, staring at
me ; but her voice trembled. ' Hav'n't I been
telling you how wicked I am? Do you think
that is a reason for His blessing me ? '

' I think His blessing has always been with
you, my poor Phebe, like the sunlight that you
try to shut out from your windows. You hide
yourself in your own darkness, and pretend

that the all-embracing love is not for you.
Well may you call your present existence a
tomb; but you must not wrong your Almighty
Father—not He, but you yourself have walled
yourself up with your own sinful hands, and
then you wonder at the weight that lies upon
your heart.'

'Can I forget my trouble when I am not
able to move?' she said bitterly. And it was
sad to see how her hands beat upon the bed-
clothes. But I held them in mine. They were
icy cold. The action seemed to calm her frenzy.

'You cannot forget,' I returned quietly;
'but all this time, all these weary years, you
might have learnt to forgive Robert.'

'Nay, I will have nothing to do with for-
giving,' was the hard answer.

'And yet you say you love him, Phebe.
Why, the very devils would laugh at such a
notion of love.'

'Didn't I say I both loved and hated him?'
very fiercely.

'Speak the truth, and say you hate him,
and God forgive you your sin. But it is a
greater one than Robert has committed against
you.'

'How dare you say such things to me, Miss Garston?' trying to free her hands; but still I held them fast. 'You will make me hate you next. I am not a pleasant-tempered woman.'

'If you do, I will promise you forgiveness beforehand. Why, you poor creature, do you think I could ever be hard on you?'

The fierce light in her eyes softened. 'Nay, I did not mean what I said; but you excite me with your talk. How can you know what I feel about these things? You cannot put yourself in my place.'

'The heart knoweth its own bitterness, Phebe; and it may be that in your place I should fail utterly in patience; but if we will not lie still under His hand, and learn the lesson He would fain teach us, it may be that fresh trials may be sent to humble us.'

'Do you think things could be much worse with me?' becoming excited again; but I stroked her hand, and begged her gently to let me finish my speech.

'Phebe, as you lie there on your cross—the whole Church throughout the world is praying for you Sunday after Sunday when the prayer goes up for those who are desolate and oppressed. And who so desolate and oppressed as you?'

'True, most true,' she murmured.

'You are cradled in the supplications of the faithful. A thousand hearts are hearing your sorrows, and yet you say impiously that you are on the borderland of hell; but no, you will never go there. There are too many marks of His love upon you. All this suffering has more meaning than that.'

It is impossible to describe the look she gave me—astonishment, incredulity, and something like dawning hope were blended in it, but she remained silent.

'You have missed your vocation, that is true. You were set apart here to do most divine work; but you have failed over it. Still you may be forgiven. How many prayers you might have prayed for Robert! You might have been an invisible shield between him and temptation. There is so much power in the prayers of unselfish love. This room, which you describe as a tomb, or an antechamber of hell, might have been an inner sanctuary, from which blessings might flow out over the whole neighbourhood. Silent

lessons of patience might have been preached
here. Your sister's weary hands might have
been strengthened. You could have mutually
consoled each other, and now——' I paused,
for here conscience completed the sentence. I
saw a tear steal under her eyelid, and then
course slowly down her face.

'I have made Susan miserable. I know that,
and she is never impatient with me if I am
ever so cross with her. Ah! I deserve my
punishment, for I have been a selfish, hateful
creature all my life. I do think sometimes that
an evil spirit lives in me.'

'There is One who can cast it out; but you
must ask Him, Phebe. Such a few words will
do: "Lord, help me!" Now we have talked
enough, and Susan will be coming back from
church. I mean to sing you the evening hymn,
and then I must go.' And almost before I had
finished the last line, Phebe, exhausted with
emotion, had sunk into a refreshing sleep, and
I crept softly out of the room to watch for
Susan's return.

I felt strangely weary as I walked home.
It was almost as though I had witnessed a
human soul struggling in the grasp of some

evil spirit. It was the first time I had ever
ministered to mental disease. Never before
had I realised what self-will, unchastened by
sorrow and untaught by religion, can bring a
woman. Once or twice that evening I had
doubted whether the brain were really un-
hinged ; but I had come to the conclusion that
it was only excess of morbid excitement.

My way home led me past the Vicarage.
Just as I was in sight of it, two figures came
out of the gate and waited to let me pass. One
of them was the churchwarden, Mr. Townsend,
and the other, Mr. Hamilton. It was impossible to avoid recognition in the bright moon-
light; but I was rather amazed when I heard
Mr. Hamilton bid Mr. Townsend good-night,
and a moment after he overtook me.

'You are out late to-night, Miss Garston.
Do you always mean to play truant from
evening service ? '

I told him how I had spent my time, but I
suppose my voice betrayed inward fatigue, for
he said, rather kindly :

'This sort of work does not suit you ; you
are looking quite pale this evening. You must
not let your feelings exhaust you. I am sorry

for Phebe myself, but she is a very tiresome
patient. Do you think you have made any
impression on her?'

He seemed rather astonished when I briefly
mentioned the subject of our talk.

'Did she tell you about herself? Come,
you have made great progress. Let her
get rid of some of the poison that seems to
choke her, and then there will be some chance
of doing her good. She has taken a great
fancy to you, that is evident; and, if you will
allow me to say so, I think you are just the
person to influence her.'

'It is a very difficult piece of work,' I returned; but he changed the subject so abruptly
that I felt convinced that he knew how utterly
jaded I was. He told me a humorous anecdote
about a child that made me laugh, and when
we reached the gate of the cottage he bade
me, rather peremptorily, put away all worrying
thoughts and to go to bed, which piece of advice
I followed as meekly as possible, after first
reading a passage out of my favourite 'Thomas
à Kempis'; but I thought of Phebe all the
time I was reading it :—

'The cross, therefore, is always ready, and

everywhere waits for thee. Thou canst not escape it whithersoever thou runnest; for whithersoever thou goest, thou carriest thyself with thee and shall ever find thyself. . . . If thou bear the cross cheerfully, it will bear thee and lead thee to the desired end, namely, where there shall be an end of suffering, though here there shall not be. If thou bear it unwillingly, thou makest for thyself a (new) burthen and increaseth thy load, and yet, notwithstanding, thou must bear it.'

CHAPTER XIII.

LADY BETTY.

THE next evening I was refused admittance to Phebe's room. Miss Locke met me at the door, looking more depressed than usual, and asked me to follow her into the kitchen, where we found Kitty in the rocking-chair by the hearth dressing her new doll.

'It is just as she treated the Vicar and Mr. Tudor,' she observed disconsolately. 'I don't quite know what ails her to-day; she had a beautiful night, and slept like a baby, and when I took her breakfast to her she put her arms round my neck and asked me to kiss her—a thing she has not done for a year or more; and she went on for a long time about

how bad she had been to me, and wanting me
to forgive her and make it up with her.'

'Well?' I demanded, rather impatiently,
as Susan wiped her patient eyes and took up
her sewing.

'Well, poor lamb! I told her I would forgive her anything and everything if she would
only let me go on with my work, for I had
Mrs. Druce's mourning to finish; but she
would not let me stir for a long time, and
cried so bitterly—though she says she never
can cry—that I thought of sending for you or
Dr. Hamilton. But she cried more when I
mentioned you, and said, No, she would not
see you; you had left her more miserable than
she was before: and she made me promise to
send you away if you came this evening, which
I am loth to do after all your kindness to
her.'

'I have brought her some fresh flowers
this evening,' was my reply. 'Do not dis-
tress yourself, Miss Locke; we must expect
Phebe to be contrary sometimes.' And the
words came to my mind, 'And ofttimes it
casteth him into the fire and oft into the
water.' 'You have discharged your duty, but

I am not going just yet. Let me help you with that work. I am very fond of sewing, and that is a nice easy piece. Shall you mind if I sing to you and Kitty a little?'

I need not have asked the question when I saw the fretted look pass from Miss Locke's face.

'It is the greatest pleasure Kitty and I have, next to going to church,' she said humbly. 'Your voice does sound so sweet; it soothes like a lullaby. It is my belief,' speaking under her breath so that the child should not hear her, 'that she is just trying to punish herself by sending you away.'

I thought perhaps this might be the case, for who could understand all the perversities of a diseased mind? But if Phebe's will was strong for evil, mine was stronger still to overcome her for her own good. I was determined on two things—first, I would not leave the house without seeing her; and, secondly, that nothing should induce me to stay with her after this reception. She must be disciplined to civility at all costs. Max had been wrong to yield to her sick whims.

I must have sung for a long time, to judge by the amount of work I contrived to do, and

if I had sung like a whole nest full of skylarks
I could not have pleased my audience more.
I was sorry to set Miss Locke's tears flowing,
because it hindered her work ; tears are such
a simple luxury, but poor folk cannot always
afford to indulge in them.

I had just commenced that beautiful song,
'Waft her, angels, through the air,' when the
impatient thumping of a stick on the floor
arrested me ; it came from Phebe's room.

' I will go to her,' I said, waving Miss Locke
back and picking up my flowers. 'Do not
look so scared, she means those knocks for me,'
and I was right in my surmise. I found her
lying very quietly, with the traces of tears still
on her face ; she addressed me quite gently.

' Do not sing any more, please ; I cannot
bear it, it makes my heart ache too much
to-night.'

' Very well,' I returned cheerfully, ' I will
just mend your fire, for it is getting low, and
put these flowers in water, and then I will bid
you good-night.'

' You are vexed with me for being rude,'
she said, almost timidly. ' I told Susan to send
you away, because I could not bear any more

talk. You made me so unhappy yesterday, Miss Garston.'

I was cruel enough to tell her that I was glad to hear it, and I must have looked as though I meant it.

'Oh, don't,' she said, shrinking as though I had dealt her a blow. 'I want you to unsay those words—they pierce me like thorns. Please tell me you did not mean them.'

'How can I know to what you are alluding?' I replied, in rather an unsympathetic tone ; but I did not intend to be soft with her to-day—she had treated me badly and must repent her ingratitude. 'I certainly meant every word I said yesterday.'

To my great surprise she burst into tears, and repeated word for word a fragment of a sentence that I had said.

'It haunts me, Miss Garston, and frightens me somehow. I have been saying it over and over in my dreams—that is what upsets me so to-day—" if we will not lie still under His hand"—yes, you said that, knowing I have never lain still for a moment—" and if we will not learn the lesson He would fain teach us, it may be that fresh trials may be sent to humble us." '

Pity kept me silent for a moment, but I knew that I must not shirk my work.

'I am sorry if the truth pains you, Phebe, but it is no less the truth; how am I to look at you and think that God has finished His work?'

She put up both her hands and motioned me away with almost a face of horror, but I took no notice. I arranged the flowers and tended the fire, and then offered her some cooling drink, which she did not refuse, and then I bade her good-night.

'What!' she exclaimed, 'are you going to leave me like that, and not a word to soothe me, after making me so unhappy? Think of the long night I have to go through.'

'Never mind the length of the night, if only you can hear His voice in the darkness. You wanted to send me away, Phebe; well, and to-morrow I shall not come; I shall stay at home and rest myself. You can send me away, and little harm will happen; but take care you do not send Him away.' And I left the room.

When I told Miss Locke that I was not coming the next evening she looked frightened.

'Has my poor Phebe offended you so badly, then?' she asked tremulously.

'I am not offended at all,' I replied; 'but Phebe has need to learn all sorts of painful lessons. I shall have all the warmer welcome on Wednesday, after leaving her to herself a little;' but Miss Locke only shook her head at this.

The next day was so lovely that I promised myself the indulgence of a long country walk; there was a pretty village about two miles from Heathfield that I longed to see again. But my little plan was frustrated, for just as I was starting I heard Tinker bark furiously; a moment afterwards there was a rush and scuffle, followed by a shriek in a girlish treble; in another moment I had seized my umbrella and flown to the door. There was a fight going on between Tinker and a large black retriever, and a little lady in brown was wandering round them helplessly wringing her hands and crying 'Oh, Nap! poor Nap!'

I took her for a child the first moment, she was so very small. 'Do not be frightened, my dear,' I said soothingly, 'I will make Tinker behave himself'—and a well-aimed blow from my umbrella made him draw off growling.

In another moment I had him by the collar, and by dint of threats and coaxing contrived to shut him up in the kitchen. He was not a quarrelsome dog generally, but, as I heard afterwards, Nap was an old antagonist; they had once fallen out about Peter, and had never been friends since.

I found the little brown girl sitting in the porch with her arms round the retriever's neck; she was kissing his black face, and begging him to forget the insult he had received from that horrid Barton dog.

'Poor old Tinker is not horrid at all, I assure you,' I said, laughing; 'he is a dear fellow, and I am already very fond of him.'

'But he nearly killed Nap,' she returned, with a little frown; 'he is worse than a savage, for he has no notion of hospitality. Nap and I came to call,' rising with an air of great dignity. 'I suppose you are Miss Garston. I am Lady Betty.'

I had never heard of such a person in Heathfield; but of course Uncle Max would enlighten me. As I looked at her more closely I saw my mistake in thinking she was a child; little brown thing as she was, she was fully grown up, and, though not in the least pretty, had a bright piquant face, a *nez retroussé*, and a pair of mischievous eyes.

She was dressed rather extravagantly in a brown velvet walking-dress, with an absurd little hat, that would have fitted a child, on the top of her dark wavy hair; she only wanted a touch of red about her to look like a magnified robin redbreast.

'Well,' she said impatiently, as I hesitated a moment in my surprise, 'I have told you we have come for a call, Nap and I; but if you are going out——'

'Oh, that is not the least consequence,' I returned, waking up to a sense of my duty. 'I am very pleased to see you and Nap; but you must not stop any longer in this cold porch; the wind is rather cutting. There is a nice fire in my parlour.' And I led the way in.

I was rather puzzled about Nap, for I seemed to recognise his sleek head and mild brown eyes; and yet where could I have seen him? He trotted in contentedly after his mistress, and stretched himself out on the rug Tinker's fashion; but Lady Betty, instead of seating herself, began to walk round the room

and inspect my books and china, making remarks upon everything in a brisk voice, and
questioning me about sundry things that attracted
her notice in rather an inquisitive manner; but,
to my great surprise and relief, she passed
Charlie's picture without remark or comment—
only I saw her glancing at it now and then
from under her long lashes. This mystified me
a little; but I thought her whole behaviour a
little peculiar. I had never before seen callers
on their first visit perambulating the room like
polar bears or throwing out curious feelers
everywhere. As a rule they sat up stiffly
enough and discussed the weather.

Lady Betty was evidently a character; most
likely she prided herself on being unlike other
people. I was just beginning to wish that she
would sit down and let me question her in my
turn, when she suddenly put up her eye-glasses
and burst into a most musical little laugh.

'Oh, do come here, Miss Garston; this is
too amusing! There goes her Majesty Gladys
of Gladwyn, accompanied by her Prime Minister.
Don't they look as though they were walking
in the Row?—heads up—everything in perfect
trim! They are coming to call—yes!—no!

They are going to the Cockaignes first—what an escape! my dear creature, if they come here I shall fly to Mrs. Barton. The Prime Minister's airs will be too much for my gravity.'

I gave her a very divided attention, for I was watching Miss Hamilton and her companion with much interest. I could see that Miss Darrell was chatting volubly; but Miss Hamilton's face looked as grave and impassive as it had looked on Sunday. When they had passed out of sight I turned to Lady Betty rather eagerly; she had dropped her eyeglasses, but an amused smile still played round her lips.

'*La belle cousine* is improving the occasion as usual. Poor Gladys, how bored she looks! but there is no escape for her this afternoon, for the Prime Minister has her in tow. I wonder from what text she is preaching? Ezekiel's dry bones, I should think, from her Majesty's face.'

'Do you know the Hamiltons of Gladwyn very intimately?' I asked innocently; but I grew rather out of patience when Lady Betty first lifted her eye-glass and stared at me, with the air of a non-comprehending kitten, and then buried her face in a very fluffy little muff in a fit of uncontrolled merriment.

I was provoked by this, and determined not to say a word. So presently she came out of her muff and asked me, with mirthful eyes, for whom I took her.'

'You are Lady Betty, I understood,' was my stiff response.

'Yes, of course; every one calls me that, except the Vicar, who will address me as Miss Elizabeth. I never will answer to that name; I hate it so. The servants up at Gladwyn never dare to use it. I would get Etta to dismiss them if they did. Is it not a shame that people should not have a voice in the matter of their name— that helpless infants should be abandoned to the tender mercies of some old fogey of a sponsor? Miss Garston, if I were ever to hear you address me by that name it would be the death-warrant to our friendship.'

'Let me know who you really are first, and then I will promise not to offend your peculiar prejudice.'

'Dear me!' she answered pettishly, 'you talk just like Giles. He often laughs at me and makes himself very unpleasant. But then, as I often tell him, philanthropists are not pleasant people with whom to live ; a man with a hobby is always odious. Well, Miss Garston, if you will be so prying, my name is Elizabeth Grant Hamilton ; only from a baby I have been called Lady Betty.'

'I shall remember,' I replied quietly, for really the little thing seemed quite ruffled. This was evidently more than a whim on her part. 'It would have seemed to me a liberty to use a family pet name. But of course if you wish me to do so——'

'I do wish it,' rather peremptorily ; 'that is partly why Mr. Cunliffe and I are not good friends—that, and other reasons.'

'Oh, I am sorry you do not like Uncle Max,' I said, rather impulsively ; but she drew herself up after the manner of an aggrieved pigeon. She was rather like a bright-eyed bird, with her fluffy hair and quick movements.

'Oh, I like him well enough, but I do not understand him. Men are not easy to understand. He is quiet, but he is disappointing. We must not expect perfection in this world,' finished the little lady, sententiously.

'I have never met any one half as good as

Uncle Max,' was my warm retort. 'He is the most unselfish of men.'

'Unselfish men make mistakes sometimes,' she returned dryly. 'Giles and he are great friends. He is up at Gladwyn a great deal, so is Mr. Tudor. Mr. Tudor is not a finished character, but he has good points—and one can tolerate him. There, how vexing, we were just beginning to talk comfortably, and I see the shadow of her Majesty's gown at the gate. Come, Nap, we must fly to Mrs. Barton's for refuge; *au revoir*, Miss Garston,' and kissing her little gloved hand this strangest of Lady Betties vanished, followed by the obedient Nap.

My pulses quickened a little at the prospect of seeing the beautiful face of Gladys Hamilton in my little room; but it was not she who entered first, but Miss Darrell, whose sharp incisive glance had taken in every detail of my surroundings before her faultlessly-gloved hand had released mine; and even when I turned to greet Miss Hamilton, her peculiar and somewhat toneless voice claimed my attention.

'How very fortunate,' she began, seating herself with elaborate caution with her back to the light. 'We hardly hoped to find you at home, Miss Garston. My cousin Giles informed us how much engaged you were. We have been so interested in what Mr. Cunliffe told us about it. It is such a romantic scheme, and, as I am a very romantic person, you may be sure of my sympathy. Gladys, dear, is this not a charming room? Positively you have so altered and beautified it that I can hardly believe it is the same room. I told a friend of ours, Mrs. Saunders, that it would never suit her, as it was such a shabby little place.'

'It is very nice,' returned Miss Hamilton, quietly. 'I hope,' fixing her large, beautiful eyes on me, 'that you are comfortable here? We thought, perhaps, you might be a little dull.'

'I have no time to be dull,' I returned, smiling, but Miss Darrell interrupted me.

'No, of course not; busy people are never dull. I told you so, Gladys, as we walked up the road. Depend upon it, I said, Miss Garston will hardly have a minute to give to our idle chatter. She will be wanting to get to her sick people, and wish us at Hanover. Still, as my cousin Giles said, we must do the right thing and call, though I am sure you are not a conventional person, neither am I—oh, we are quite kindred souls here.'

I tried to receive this speech in good part, but I certainly protested inwardly against the notion that Miss Darrell and I would ever be kindred souls. I felt an instinctive repugnance to her voice : its want of tone jarred on me ; and all the time she talked, her hard, bright eyes seemed to dart restlessly from Miss Hamilton to me. I felt sure that nothing could escape their scrutiny, but now and then, when one looked at her in return, she seemed to veil them most curiously under the long curling lashes.

She was rather an elegant-looking woman, but her face was decidedly plain. She had thin lips and rather a square jaw, and her sallow complexion lacked colour. One could not guess her age exactly, but she might have been three or four and thirty. I heard her spoken of afterwards as a very interesting-looking person ; certainly her figure was fine, and she knew how to dress herself—a very useful art when women have no claim to beauty.

Miss Darrell's voluble tongue seemed to touch

on every subject.   Miss Hamilton sat perfectly
silent, and I had not a chance of addressing her.
Once, when I looked at her, I could see her eyes
were fixed on my darling's picture.   She was
gazing at it with an air of absorbed melancholy; her lips were firmly closed, and her
hands lay folded in her lap.

'That is the picture of my twin brother,'
I said softly, to arouse her.

To my surprise she turned paler than ever,
and her lips quivered.

' Your twin brother, yes—and you have lost
him ? ' But here Miss Darrell chimed in again—

'How very interesting !   What a blessing
photography is, to be sure !   Do you take well,
Miss Garston ?   They make me a perfect fright.
I tell my cousins that nothing on earth will
induce me to try another sitting.   Why should
I endure such a martyrdom, if it be not to give
pleasure to my friends ? '

To my surprise, Miss Hamilton's voice interrupted her—it was a little like her step-
brother's voice, and had a slight hesitation that
was not in the least unpleasant.   She spoke
rather slowly : at least it seemed so by comparison with Miss Darrell's quick sentences.

s 2

'Etta, we have not done what Giles told us. We hope you will come and dine with us to-morrow, Miss Garston, without any ceremony.'

'Dear me, how careless of me,' broke in Miss Darrell, but her forehead contracted a little, as though her cousin's speech annoyed her. 'Giles gave the message to me, but we were talking so fast that I quite forgot it. My cousin will have it that you are dull, and our society may cheer you up. I do not hold with Giles. I think you are far too superior a person to be afraid of a little solitude ; strong-minded people like you are generally fond of their own society ; but all the same, I hope you do not mean to be quite a recluse.'

'We dine at seven, but I hope you will come as much earlier as you like,' interposed Miss Hamilton. 'No one will be with us but Mr. Tudor.'

'You forget Mr. Cunliffe, Gladys,' observed Miss Darrell, in rather a sharp voice. 'I am sure I do not know what the poor man has done to offend you ; but ever since last summer——' But here Miss Hamilton rose with a gesture that was almost queenly, and her impassive face looked graver than ever.

'I did not know you had invited Mr. Cunliffe, Etta, or I should certainly have mentioned him. Good-bye, Miss Garston; we shall look for you soon after six.'

There was something wistful in her expression; it seemed as though she wanted me to come, and yet I was a complete stranger to her. I felt very reluctant to dine at Gladwyn, but that look overruled me.

'I will try to come early,' was my answer, and then I drew back to let them pass.

Miss Darrell bade me good-bye a little stiffly—something had evidently put her out; as they went down the narrow garden path I could see she was speaking to Miss Hamilton rather angrily, but Miss Hamilton seemed to take no notice.

What did it all mean? I wondered; and then I suddenly bethought myself of my other visitor. I had wholly forgotten her existence in my interest in her beautiful sister. What could have become of Lady Betty?

CHAPTER XIV.

LADY BETTY LEAVES HER MUFF.

THIS question was speedily answered.

The gate had scarcely closed behind my visitors when I heard a gay little laugh behind me, and Lady Betty tripped across the passage, and took possession of the easy-chair in the friendliest way.

'Now we can have a chat and be cosy all by ourselves,' she said, with childish glee; and then she stopped and looked at me, and her rosy little mouth began to pout, and a sort of baby frown came to her forehead.

'You don't seem pleased to see me again; shall I go away? Are you busy or tired, or is there anything the matter?' asked Lady Betty, in an extremely fractious voice.

'There is nothing the matter, and I am

delighted to see you, and—' with a sudden in-
spiration, 'if you will be good enough to stay
and have tea with me I will ask Mrs. Barton
to send in one of her excellent tea-cakes.'

This was evidently what Lady Betty
wanted, for she nodded and took off her hat,
and began to unbutton her long tan-coloured
gloves in a cool businesslike way that amused
me. I ran across to the kitchen, and gave
Mrs. Barton a *carte blanche* for a sumptuous tea,
and when I returned I found Lady Betty quite
divested of her walking apparel, and patting
her dark fluffy hair to reduce it to some degree
of smoothness. She had a pretty little head,
and it was covered by a mass of short curly
hair that nothing would reduce to order.

'This is just what I like,' she said promptly.
'When Giles told us about you, and I made up
my mind to call, I hoped you would ask me to
stay. I do dislike stiffness and conventionality
excessively. I hope you mean to be friends
with us, Miss Garston, for I have taken rather
a fancy to you, in spite of your grave looks.
Dear me, do you always look so grave?'

'Oh, no,' I returned, laughing.

'That is right,' with an approving nod;

'you look ever so much nicer and younger when you smile. Well, what did the Prime Minister say? Was she very gushing and sympathetic? Did she patronise you in a ladylike way, and pat you on the head metaphorically, until you felt ready to box her ears? Ah, I know *la belle cousine's* little ways?'

This was so exact a description of my conversation with Miss Darrell that I laughed in a rather guilty fashion. Lady Betty clapped her hands delightedly.

'Oh, I have found you out. You are not a bit solemn, really, only you put on the airs of a sister of mercy. So you don't like Etta; you need not be afraid of telling me so; she is the greatest humbug in the world, only Giles is so foolish as to believe in her. I call her a humbug because she pretends to be what she is not; she is really a most prosaic sort of person, and she wants to make people believe that she is a soft romantic body.'

'You are not very charitable in your estimate of your cousin, Lady Betty.'

'Then she should not lead Gladys such a life—poor dear Majesty, to be ruled by her

Prime Minister. I should like to see Etta try to dictate to me. Why, I should laugh in her face. She would not attempt it again. I can't think how it is,' looking a little grave, ' that she has Gladys so completely under her thumb. Gladys is too proud to own that she is afraid of her, but all the same she never dares to act in opposition to Etta.'

Lady Betty's confidence was rather embarrassing, but I hardly knew how to check it. I began to think the household at Gladwyn must be a very queer one. Uncle Max had already hinted at a want of harmony between Mr. Hamilton and his step-sisters, and Miss Darrell seemed hardly a favourite with him, although he was too kind-hearted to say so openly.

' Has your cousin lived long with you ? ' I ventured to ask.

' Oh, yes; ever since Gladys and I were little things; before mamma died. Auntie lived with us too—poor auntie, we were very fond of her, but she was a sad invalid ; she died about three years ago. Etta has managed everything ever since.'

' Do you mean that Miss Darrell is house-

keeper? I should have thought that would
have been your sister's place.'

'Oh, Gladys is called the mistress of the
house, but none of the servants go to her for
orders. If she gives any, Etta is sure to
countermand them.'

'It is partly Gladys' fault,' went on Lady
Betty, in her frank outspoken way. 'She tried
for a little while to manage things; but either
she was a terribly bad housekeeper, or Etta
undermined her influence in the house; but
everything went wrong, and Giles got so angry
—men do, you know, when the dear creatures'
comforts are invaded—so there was a great
fuss, and Gladys gave it up; and now the
Prime Minister manages the finances, and gives
out stores, and though I hate to say it, things
never went more smoothly than they do now.
Giles is scarcely ever vexed.'

I am ashamed to say how much I was interested in Lady Betty's childish talk, and yet
I knew it was wrong not to check her. What
would Miss Hamilton say if she were to hear of
our conversation? Jill was rather a reckless
talker, but she was nothing compared with this
daring little creature. Lady Betty told me

afterwards, when we were better acquainted, that it had amused her so to see how widely I could open my eyes when I was surprised. I believe she did it out of pure mischief.

Our talk was happily interrupted by the appearance of Mrs. Barton and the tea-tray, which at once turned Lady Betty's thoughts into a new channel.

There was so much to do. First she must help to arrange the table, and as no one else could cut such thin bread and butter she must try her hand at that. Then Nap must have his tea before we touched ours; and when at last we did sit down she was praising the cake, and jumping up for the kettle, and waiting upon me 'because I was a dear good thing, and waited on poor people,' and coaxing me to take this or that as though I were her guest, and every now and then she paused to say 'how nice and cosy it was,' and how she was enjoying herself, and how glad she felt to miss that stupid dinner at Gladwyn, where no one talked but Giles and Etta, and Gladys sat as though she were half asleep, until she, Lady Betty, felt inclined to pinch them all.

We were approaching the dangerous sub-

ject again, but I warded it off, by asking how
she and her sister employed their time.

She made a little face at me, as though the
question bothered her. 'Oh, I do things—and
Gladys—does things,' rather lucidly.

'Well, but what things, may I ask?'

'Why do you want to know?' was the
unexpected retort. 'I don't question you, do
I? Giles says women are dreadfully curious.'

'I think you are dreadfully mysterious; but
as you are evidently ashamed of your occupa-
tions, I will withdraw my question.'

'I do believe you are cross, Miss Garston—
you are not a saint after all, though Giles says
you sing like a cherub—I don't know where
he ever heard one, but that is his affair. Well,
as you choose to get pettish over it, I will be
amiable, and tell you what we do. Etta says
we waste our time dreadfully, but as it is our
time and not hers, it is none of her business.'

I thought it prudent to remain silent, so
she wrinkled her brows and looked perplexed.

'Gladys—let me see what Gladys does:
well, she used to teach in the schools, but she
does not teach now—she says the infants make
her head ache, that is why she has dropped

the Sunday school. Now Etta has her class.
Then there was the mothers' meeting; well, I
never knew why she gave that up—I wonder
if she knows herself—but Etta has got it; and
she has left off singing at the penny readings
and village entertainments—Etta would have
replaced her there, only she has no voice. I
think she works a little for the poor people at
the East End of London, but she does it in her
own room, because Etta laughs at her and
calls her " Madam Charity." Gladys hates that.
She takes long walks, and sketches a little and
reads a good deal; and there, that is all I
know of her Majesty's doings.'

Poor Miss Hamilton; it certainly did not
sound much of a life.

'And about yourself, Lady Betty.'

'Oh ! Lady Betty is here, there, and everywhere,' mimicking me in a droll way. 'Lady
Betty walks a little, talks a little, plays a little,
and dances when she gets a chance. At present, lawn-tennis is a great object in her life;
last winter, swimming in Brill's bath and riding
from Hove to Kemp Town or across the Brighton Downs were her hobbies. In the summer a
gardening craze seized her, and just now she

is in an idle mood. What does it matter? a short life and a merry one—eh, Miss Garston!'

I would not expostulate with this civilised little heathen, for she was evidently bent on provoking a lecture, and I determined to disappoint her. We had sat so long over our tea that the room was quite dark, and I rose to kindle the lamp. Lady Betty, as usual, was anxious to assist me, and went to the window to lower the blind. The next moment I heard an exclamation of annoyance, and as she came back to the table her little brown face was all aglow with some suppressed irritation.

'What is the matter, Lady Betty?' I asked, in some surprise.

'It is that provoking Etta again,' she began. 'She has guessed where I am, and has sent for me, the meddlesome old——' But here a tap at our room door stopped her outburst.

As Lady Betty made no response, I said 'Come in,' and immediately a respectable-looking woman appeared in the doorway.

She looked like a superior lady's-maid, and had a plain face much marked by the small-pox, and rather dull light-coloured eyes.

'Well, Leah,' demanded Lady Betty,

rather sulkily, 'what is your business with Miss Garston ?'

'My business is with you, Lady Betty,' returned the woman, good-humouredly. 'Master came in just now and asked where you were —I think he told Miss Darrell that it was too late for you to be out walking; so Miss Darrell said she believed you were at the White Cottage, for she saw your muff lying on Miss Garston's table ; so she told me to step up here, as it was too dark for you to walk alone, and I was to tell you that they would be waiting dinner.'

'It is just like her interference,' muttered Lady Betty. 'But I suppose there would be a pretty fuss if I let the dinner spoil. Help me on with my jacket, Leah ; as you have come when no one wanted you, you had better make yourself useful.'

She spoke with the peremptoriness of a spoiled child, but the woman smiled pleasantly and did as she was bid. She seemed a civil sort of person, evidently an old family servant. Something had struck me in her speech. Miss Darrell had seen Lady Betty's muff, and knew of her presence in the cottage, and yet she had made no remark on the subject; this seemed strange, but would she not wonder still more at my silence?

'Lady Betty,' I said hastily as this occurred to me; 'your cousin will think it odd that I never spoke of you this afternoon; but you ran out of the room so quickly, and then I forgot all about it.'

'Oh, Etta will know I was only playing at hide-and-seek. Most likely she will think I bound you to secrecy. What a goose I was to leave my muff behind me—the very one Etta gave me, too; why, she would see a pin, nothing escapes her—does it, Leah?'

'Not much, Lady Betty—she has fine eyes for dust, I tell her. The new housemaid had better be careful with her room; now, ma'am, if you are ready?'

'Good-bye, Miss Garston; we shall meet to morrow,' returned Lady Betty, standing on tiptoe to kiss me, and as they went out I heard her say in quite a friendly manner to Leah, as though she had already forgotten her grievance—

'Is not Miss Garston nice, Leah? She has got such a kind face.' But I did not hear Leah's reply.

I had not seen the last of my visitors, for about an hour afterwards, as I was finishing a long chatty letter to Jill, there was the sharp click of the gate again, and Uncle Max came in.

'Are you busy, Ursula?' he said apologetically, as I looked up in some surprise. 'I only called in as I was passing. I am going on to the Myers's—old Mr. Myers is ill and wants to see me.' But for all that Max drew his accustomed chair to the fire, and looked at the blazing pine-knot a little dreamily.

'You keep good fires,' was his next remark. 'It is very cold to-night, there is a touch of frost in the air—Tudor was saying so just now. So you have had the ladies from Gladwyn here this afternoon.'

'How do you know that?' I asked in a sharp pouncing voice, for I was keeping that bit of news for a tit-bit.

'Oh, I met them,' he returned absently, 'and they told me that you were to dine with them to-morrow. I call that nice and friendly, asking you without ceremony. What time shall you be ready, Ursula, for of course I shall not let you go alone the first time?'

I was glad to hear this, for though I was

not a shy person my first visit to Gladwyn would be a little formidable; so I told him briefly that I would be ready by half past six, as they wished me to go early, and it would never do to be formal on my side. And then I gave him an account of Lady Betty's visit, but it did not seem to interest him much; in fact, I do not believe that he listened very attentively.

'She is an odd little being,' he said rather absently, 'and prides herself on being as unconventional as possible. They have spoiled her among them, Hamilton especially, but her droll ways amuse him. She has sulked with me lately because I will not give in to her absurd fad about Lady Betty. I tell her that she ought not to be ashamed of her baptismal name; the angels will call her by it one day.'

'She is very amusing. I think I shall like her, Max; but Miss Darrell does not please me. She is far too gushing and talkative for my taste; she patronised and repressed me in the same breath. If there is anything I dislike it is to be patted on the head by a stranger.'

'Miss Hamilton did not pat you on the head, I suppose?'

'Miss Hamilton! Oh dear no, she is of

another calibre. I have quite fallen in love
with her, her face is perfect, only rather too
pale, and her manners are so gentle, and yet
she has plenty of dignity ; she reminds me of
Clyte, only her expression is not so contented
and restful—she looks far too melancholy for a
girl of her age.'

'Pshaw !' he said, rather impatiently, but I
noticed he looked uncomfortable. 'What can
have put such ideas in your head?—you have
only seen her twice—you could not expect her
to smile in church.'

Max seemed so thoroughly put out by my
remark that I thought it better to qualify my
speech. 'Most likely Miss Darrell had been
nagging at her.'

His face cleared up directly. 'Depend
upon it that was the reason she looked so
grave,' he said with an air of relief. 'Miss
Darrell can say ill-tempered things sometimes.
Miss Hamilton is never as lively as Miss Elizabeth ; she is always quiet and thoughtful ; some
girls are like that, they are not sparkling and
frothy.'

I let him think that I accepted this statement as gospel, but in my heart I thought I

T 2

had never seen a sadder face than that of
Gladys Hamilton; to me it looked absolutely
joyless, as though some strange blight had
fallen on her youth. I kept these thoughts
to myself like a wise woman, and when Max
looked at me rather searchingly as though he
expected a verbal assent, I said: 'Yes, you
are right, some girls are like that,' and left
him to glean my meaning out of this parrot-
like sentence.

I could make nothing of Max this evening,
he seemed restless and ill at ease; now and
then he fell into a brown study and roused
himself with difficulty. I was almost glad
when he took his leave at last, for I had a
feeling somehow—and a curious feeling it was
—that we were talking at cross purposes, and
that our speeches seemed to be lost hopelessly
in a mental fog; the cipher to our meaning
seemed missing.

But he bade me good-night as affectionately
as though I had done him a world of good;
and when he had gone I sat down to my piano
and sang all my old favourite songs, until the
lateness of the hour warned me to extinguish
my lamp and retire to bed.

I was just sinking into a sweet sleep when I heard Nathaniel's voice bidding some one good-night, and in another moment I could hear firm quick footsteps down the gravel walk followed by Nap's joyous bark.

Mr. Hamilton had been in the house all the time I had been amusing myself—I do not know why the idea annoyed me so. "'How I wish he would keep away sometimes,' I thought fretfully; ' he will think I am practising for to-morrow ; I will not sing if they press me to do so.' And with this ill-natured resolve I fell asleep.

My dinner engagement obliged me to go to Phebe quite early in the afternoon. Miss Locke looked surprised as she opened the door, but she greeted me with a pleased smile.

' Phebe will hardly be looking for you yet,' she said, leading the way into the kitchen in the evident expectation of a chat; ' she did finely yesterday in spite of her missing you; when I went in to her in the morning she quite took my breath away by asking if there were not an easier chair in the house for you to use. "'Deed, and there is Phebe woman," I said, quite pleased, for the poor thing is far too uncomfortable herself to look after other people's comforts, and it was such a new thing to hear her speak like that, so I fetched father's big elbow-chair with a cushion or two and his little wooden footstool, and there it stands ready for you this afternoon.'

'That was very thoughtful of Phebe,' was my reply.

'Well, now, I thought you would be pleased, though it is only a trifle. But that is not all. Widow Drayton was sitting with me last afternoon, when all at once she puts up her finger and says, "Hark! Is not that your Kitty's voice?" And so I stole out into the passage to listen. And there, to be sure, was Kitty singing most beautifully some of the hymns you sang to Phebe; and if she could not make out all the words she just went on with the tune, like a little bird, and Phebe lay and listened to her, and all the time—as I could see through the crack of the door—her eyes were fixed on the picture you gave her, and I said to myself, "Phebe, woman, this is as it should be. You may yet learn wisdom out of the lips of babes and sucklings."'

'I am very glad to hear all this, Miss

Locke,' I returned cheerfully. 'Kitty will be able to take my place sometimes. She will be a valuable little ally; now, as my time is limited, I will go to Phebe.'

I was much struck by the changed expression on Phebe's face as soon as I had entered the room. She certainly looked very ill, and when I questioned her avowed she had suffered a good deal of pain in the night; but the wild hard look had left her eyes. There was intense depression, but that was all.

She evidently enjoyed the singing as much as ever; and I took care to sing my best. When I had finished I produced a story that I thought suitable, and began to read to her. She listened for about half an hour before she showed a symptom of weariness. At the first sign I stopped.

'Will you do something to please me in return?' I asked, when she had thanked me very civilly. 'I want you to go on with this book by yourself now. I know what you are going to say—that you never read; that it makes your head ache and tires you. But if you care to please me you will waive all these objections, and we can talk over the story to-morrow.' Then I told her about my invitation for this evening, and about the beautiful Miss Hamilton, whose sweet face had interested me. And when we had chatted quite comfortably for a little while I rose to take my leave.

Of course, she could not let me go without one sharp little word.

'You have been kinder to me to-day,' she said, pausing slightly. 'I suppose that is because I let you take your own way with me.'

'Every one likes his own way,' I said lightly. 'If I have been kinder to you, as you say, possibly it is because you have deserved kindness more.' And I smiled at her and patted the thin hand, as though she were a child; and so 'went on my way rejoicing,' as they say in the good old Book.

CHAPTER XV.

UP AT GLADWYN.

UNCLE MAX had never been famous for punctuality. He was slightly Bohemian in his habits, and rather given to desultory bachelor ways; but his domestic timekeeper, Mrs. Drabble, ruled him most despotically in the matter of meals, and it was amusing to see how she kept him and Mr. Tudor in order—neither of them ventured to keep the dinner waiting for fear of the housekeeper's black looks—such an offence they knew would be expiated by cold fish and burnt-up steaks. Uncle Max might invite the Bishop to dine, but if his lordship chose to be late Mrs. Drabble would take no pains to keep her dinner hot.

'If gentlemen like to shilly-shally with their food, they must take things as they find them,' she would say ; and if her master ever ventured to remonstrate with her, she took care that he should suffer for it for a week.

'We must humour Mother Drabble,' Mr. Tudor would say good-humouredly, 'every one has a crotchet, and after all she is a worthy little woman, and makes us very comfortable. I never knew what good cooking meant until I came to the Vicarage ; ' and indeed Mrs. Drabble's custards and flaky crust were famed in the village. Miss Darrell had once begged very humbly that her cook Parker might take a lesson from her, but Mrs. Drabble refused pointblank.

'There were those who liked to teach others and plenty of them, but she was one who minded her own business and kept her own receipts. If Miss Darrell wanted a custard made she was willing to do it for her and welcome, but she wanted no gossiping prying cooks about her kitchen.'

As I knew Max's peculiarity, I was somewhat surprised when, long before the appointed time, Mrs. Barton came up and told me that

Mr. Cunliffe was in the parlour. I had commenced my toilet in rather a leisurely fashion,
but now I made haste to join him, and ran
downstairs as quickly as possible, carrying my
fur-lined cloak over my arm.

'You look very nice, my dear,' he said in
quite a fatherly fashion; ' have I ever seen that
gown before ? '

The gown in point had been given to me
by Lesbia, and had been made in Paris; it was
one of those thin black materials that make
up into a charming demi-toilette, and was a
favourite gown with me.

I always remember the speech Lesbia made
as she showed it to me. ' When you put on
this gown, Ursula, you must think of the poor
little woman who hoped to have been your
sister.' This was one of the pretty little
speeches that she often made. Poor dear
Lesbia! she always did things so gracefully.
In Charlie's lifetime I had thought her cold
and frivolous, for she had not then folded up
her butterfly wings; but even then she was
always doing kind little things.

It was a dark night, neither moon nor stars
to be seen, and after we had passed the church

the darkness seemed to envelop us, and I could barely distinguish the path. Max seemed quite oblivious of this fact, for he would persist in pointing out invisible objects of interest. I was told of the wide stretch of country that lay on the right, and how freshly the soft breezes blew over the downs.

'There is the asylum, Ursula,' he observed cheerfully, waving his hand towards the black outline. 'Now we are passing Colonel Maberley's house, and here is Gladwyn. I wish you could have seen it by daylight.'

I wished so, too, for on entering the shrubbery the darkness seemed to swallow us up bodily, and the heavy oak door might have belonged to a prison. The sharp clang of the bell made me shiver, and Dante's lines came into my mind rather inopportunely, 'All ye who enter here, leave hope behind.' But as soon as the door opened the scene was changed like magic; the long hall was deliciously warm and light: it looked almost like a corridor, with its dark marble figures holding sconces, and small carved tables between them.

'I will wait for you here, Ursula,' whispered Uncle Max; and I went off in charge of the

same maid that I had seen before. Lady Betty
had called her Leah, and as I followed her upstairs I thought of that tender-eyed Leah who
had been an unloved wife.

Leah was very civil, but I thought her
manner bordered on familiarity; perhaps she
had lived long in the family, and was treated
more as a friend than a servant. She was an
exceedingly plain young woman, and her light
eyes had a curious lack of expression in them,
and yet, like Miss Darrell's, they seemed able
to see everything.

Seeing me glance round the room—it was
a large, handsomely furnished bed-room, with a
small dressing-room attached to it—she said,
'This is Miss Darrell's room. Mrs. Darrell used
to occupy it, and Miss Etta slept in the dressing-
room, but ever since her mother's death she
has had both rooms.'

'Indeed,' was my brief reply; but I could
not help thinking that Miss Darrell had very
pleasant and roomy quarters. There were
evidences of luxury everywhere, from the
bevelled glass of the walnutwood wardrobe
to the silver-mounted dressing-case and ivory
brushes on the toilet table. A pale embroidered

tea-gown lay across the couch, and a book that looked very much like a French novel was thrown beside it. Miss Darrell was evidently a Sybarite in her tastes.

Uncle Max was waiting for me at the foot of the stairs, and took me into the drawing-room at once.

To our surprise we found Miss Hamilton there alone. The room was only dimly lighted, and she was sitting in a large carved chair beside the fire with an open book in her lap.

I wonder if Max noticed how like a picture she looked. She was dressed very simply in a soft creamy cashmere, and her fair hair was piled up on her head in regal fashion: the smooth plaits seemed to crown her; a little knot of red berries that had been carelessly fastened against her throat was the only colour about her; but she looked more like Clyte than ever, and again I told myself that I had never seen a sweeter face.

She greeted me with gentle warmth, but she hardly looked at Max; her white lids dropped over her eyes whenever he addressed her, and when she answered him she seemed to speak in a more measured voice than usual.

Max too appeared extremely nervous; instead of sitting down, he stood upon the bearskin rug, and fidgeted with some tiny Chinese ornaments on the mantelpiece. Neither of them appeared at ease—was it possible that they were not friends?

'You are not often to be found in solitude, Miss Hamilton,' observed Max, and it struck me his voice was a little peculiar. 'I do not think I have ever seen you sitting alone in this room before.'

'No,' she answered quickly, and then she went on in rather a hesitating manner: 'Etta and Lady Betty have been shopping in Brighton, and they came back by a late train, and now Etta is shut up with Giles in his study. Some letters that came by this morning's post had to be answered.'

'Miss Darrell is Hamilton's secretary, is she not?'

'She writes a good many of his letters. Giles is rather idle about correspondence, and she helps him with his business and accounts. Etta is an extremely busy person.'

'Miss Hamilton used to be busy too,' returned Max, quietly. 'I always considered you an example to our ladies. I lost one of my best workers when I lost you.'

A painful colour came into Miss Hamilton's face.

'Oh no!' she protested rather feebly. 'Etta is far cleverer than I at parish work. Teaching does not make her head ache.'

'Yours used not to ache last summer,' persisted Uncle Max, but she did not seem to hear him. She had turned to me, and there was almost an appealing look in her beautiful eyes, as though she were begging me to talk.

'Oh, do you know, Miss Garston,' she said nervously, 'that Giles was very nearly sending for you last night? He was with Mrs. Blagrove's little girl until five this morning; the poor little creature died at half past four, and he told us that he thought half a dozen times of sending for you.'

'I wish he had done so. I should have been so glad to help.'

'Yes, he knew that, but he said it would have been such a shame rousing you out of your warm bed; and he had not the heart to do it. So he stopped on himself, there was really nothing to be done; but the parents were

in such a miserable state, that he did not like
to leave them ; he was so tired this afternoon
that he dropped asleep instead of writing his
letters, that is why Etta has to do them.'

' Who is talking about Etta ? ' observed Miss
Darrell, coming in that moment, with a quick
rustle of her silk skirt, looking as well dressed,
self-possessed, and full of assurance as ever.
' Why are you good people sitting in the dark ?
Thornton would have lighted the candles if
you had rung, Gladys ; but I suppose you forgot,
and were dreaming over the fire as usual.
Miss Garston, I suppose I ought to apologise
for being late, but we are such busy people
here—every moment is of value ; and though
Gladys asked you to come early, I never
thought you would be so good as to do so.
Friendly people are scarce, are they not, Mr.
Cunliffe ? By the bye,' holding up a taper finger
loaded with sparkling rings, ' I have a scolding in store for you. Why did you not examine
my class as usual last Sunday ?—the children
tell me you never came near them.'

' I had so little time that I asked Tudor to
take the classes for me,' he returned quickly,
but he was looking at Miss Hamilton as he

spoke. 'I am always sure of the children in that class—they have been so thoroughly well taught that there is very little need for me to interfere.'

'It would encourage their teachers if you were to do so,' returned Miss Darrell, smiling graciously. She evidently appropriated the praise to herself, but I am sure Uncle Max was not thinking of her when he spoke. Just then Lady Betty came into the room followed by Mr. Tudor.

Lady Betty looked almost pretty to-night. She wore a dark ruby velveteen that exactly suited her brown skin; her fluffy hair was tolerably smooth, and she had a bright colour. She came and sat down beside me at once.

'Oh! I am so vexed that we are so late; but it was all Etta's fault—she would look in at every shop window, and so of course we lost the proper train.'

'What does the child say?' asked Miss Darrell, good-humouredly. She seemed in excellent spirits this evening—but how silent Miss Hamilton had become since her entrance. 'Of course poor Etta is blamed, she always is if anything goes wrong in the house; Etta is the family scapegoat; but who was it, I wonder, who wanted another turn on the pier—not Etta, certainly ? '

'Just as though those few minutes would have mattered, and I did want another look at the sea,' returned Lady Betty, pettishly ; ' but no, you preferred those stupid shops, that is why I hate to go into Brighton with you.' But Miss Darrell only laughed at this flimsy display of wrath.

Just then Mr. Tudor had taken the other vacant chair beside me. ' How is the village nurse ? ' he asked in his bright way.

I certainly liked Mr. Tudor ; he had such a pleasant, friendly way with him, and on his part he seemed always glad to see me. If I had ever talked slang, I might have said that we chummed together famously. He was a year younger than myself, and I took advantage of this to give him advice in an elder-sisterly fashion.

' You must take care that the clergy do not spoil the village nurse,' observed Miss Darrell, who had overheard him, and this time the taper finger was uplifted against Mr. Tudor.

' Oh, there is no fear of that,' he returned

manfully; 'Miss Garston is too sensible to allow herself to be spoiled; but it is quite right that we all should make much of her.'

'We will ask Giles if he agrees with this,' replied Miss Darrell, in a funny voice, and at that moment Mr. Hamilton entered the room.

I do not know why I thought he looked nicer that evening—one thing, I had never seen him in evening dress, and it suited him better than his rough tweed; he was quieter and less abrupt in manner, more dignified and less peremptory, but he certainly looked very tired.

He accosted me rather gravely, I thought, though he said that he was glad to see me at Gladwyn. His first remark after this was to complain of the lateness of the dinner.

'Parker is not very punctual this evening, Etta,' he observed, looking at his watch.

'I think it was our fault, Giles,' returned his cousin, plaintively. 'We kept Thornton such a long time in the study, and no doubt that is the cause of the delay. Parker is seldom a minute behindhand; punctuality is her chief point, as Mrs. Edmonstone told me when I engaged her. You see,' turning to Uncle Max,

' we are such a regular household that the least deviation in our nature quite throws us into confusion. I am so sorry, Giles, I am, indeed; but will you ring for Thornton, and that will remind him of his duty.'

Miss Darrell's submissive speech evidently disarmed Mr. Hamilton, and deprived him of his Englishman's right to grumble to his womankind; so he said, quite amiably, that they would wait for Parker's pleasure a little longer, and then relapsed into silence.

The next moment I saw him looking at me with rather an odd expression; it was as though he were regarding a stranger whom he had not seen before—I suppose the term ' taking stock' would explain my meaning. Just then dinner was announced, and he gave me his arm.

The dining-room was very large and lofty, and was furnished in dark oak. A circular seat with velvet cushions ran round the deep bay window. A small oval table stood before it. Dark ruby curtains closed in the bay.

My first speech to Mr. Hamilton was to regret that he had not sent for me the previous night.

'Oh, no!' he said pleasantly. 'I am quite glad now that your rest was not disturbed.' And then he went on looking at me with the same queer expression that his face had worn before.

'Do you know, Miss Garston, your remark quite startled me? Somehow I do not seem to recognise my nurse to-night. When I came into the drawing-room just now I thought there was a strange young lady sitting by Tudor.'

Of course I was curious to know what he meant; but he positively refused to enlighten me, and went on speaking about his poor little patient.

'She was an only child; but nothing could have saved her. The Blagroves are well-to-do people—Brighton shopkeepers—so they hardly come under the category of your patients. Miss Garston, you call yourself a servant of the poor, do you not?'

'I should not refuse to help any one who really needed it,' was my reply. 'But, of course, if people can afford to hire service, I should think my labour thrown away on them.'

'Ah! just so. But now and then we meet with a case where hirelings can give no com-

fort. With the Blagroves, for example, there
was nothing to be done but just to watch the
child's feeble life ebb away. A miracle only
could have saved her; but all the same, it was
impossible to go away and leave them. They
were young people, and had never seen death
before.'

I was surprised to hear him speak with so
much feeling. And I liked that expression
'servant of the poor.' It sounded to me as
though he had at last grasped my meaning,
and that I had nothing more to fear from his
sarcasm.

I wondered what had wrought such a
sudden change in him, for I had only worked
such a few days. Certainly, it would make
things far easier if I could secure him as an
ally; and I began to hope that we should go
on more smoothly in the future.

Mr. Hamilton was evidently a man whom
it would take long to know. His was by no
means a character easy to read. One would
be sure to be startled by new developments and
curious contradictions. I had known him only
for ten days; but then we had met constantly
in that short time. I had seen him hard in

manner and soft in speech—cool, critical, and disparaging; at one moment satirical and provoking, the next full of thoughtfulness and readiness to help. No wonder I found it difficult to comprehend him. When we had finished discussing the Blagroves, Mr. Hamilton turned his attention to his other guests, and tried to promote the general conversation ; this left me at liberty to make my own observations.

Miss Hamilton sat at the top of the table facing her brother; and Uncle Max and Mr. Tudor were beside her ; but she did not speak to either of them unless they addressed her, and her replies seemed to be very brief. If I had been less interested in her I might have accused her of want of animation, for it is hardly playing the *rôle* of a hostess to look beautiful, and be chary of words and smiles.

It was impossible to attribute her silence to absence of mind, for she followed every word that was spoken with grave attention ; but for some inexplicable reason she had withdrawn into herself. Uncle Max left her to herself after a time, and began to talk politics with Mr. Hamilton, and Mr. Tudor was soon compelled to follow his example.

Poor Mr. Tudor! I rather pitied him, for his other neighbour, Lady Betty, had turned suddenly very sulky, and I had my surmises that Miss Darrell had said something to affront her; for she made snapping little answers when any one spoke to her, and though they laughed at her, and nobody seemed to mind, most likely they thought it prudent to give her time to recover herself.

Miss Darrell's radiant good-humour was a strange contrast to her two cousins' silence. She threw herself gallantly into the breach, and talked fast and well on every topic broached by the gentlemen. She was evidently clever and well read, and had dabbled in literature and politics.

Her energy and vivacity were almost fatiguing. She seemed able to keep up two or three conversations at once. The lowest whisper did not escape her ear; if Mr. Hamilton spoke to me, I saw her watchful eye on us, and she joined in at once with a sprightly word or two; the next moment she was answering Uncle Max, who had at last hazarded a remark to his silent neighbour. Miss Hamilton had no time to reply; her cousin's laugh and ready word were before her.

I found the same thing happen when Mr. Tudor addressed me, before he had finished his sentence she had challenged the attention of the table.

'Giles,' she said good-humouredly ; 'do you know what Mr. Tudor said in the drawing-room just now, that it was the bounden duty of the Heathfield folk to spoil and make much of Miss Garston ? '

Both Mr. Tudor and I looked confused at this audacious speech, but he tried to defend himself as well as he could.

'No, no, Miss Darrell, that was not quite what I said ; the whole style of the sentence is too laboured to belong to me—" bounden duty," no, it does not sound like me at all.'

'We need not quarrel about terms,' she persisted, 'your meaning was just the same. Come, Mr. Tudor, you cannot unsay your own words, that it was right for you all to make much of Miss Garston.'

I thought this was spoken in the worst possible taste, and I am sure Mr. Hamilton thought so too, for he smiled slightly and said, 'Nonsense, Etta, you let your tongue run away with you. I daresay that was not Tudor's meaning at all; he is the most matter-of-fact fellow I know, and could not coin a compliment to save his life. Besides which I expect he has found out by this time that it would be rather difficult to spoil Miss Garston—that cuts both ways, eh!' looking at me rather mischievously.

'Oh! if all the gentlemen are in conspiracy to defend Miss Garston, I will say no more,' returned Miss Darrell, with a shrug, but she did not say it quite pleasantly. 'Gladys dear, I think we had better retire before I am quite crushed; Giles's frown has quite flattened me out. Miss Garston, if you are ready,' making me a mocking little curtsy; but Miss Hamilton waited for me at the door .and linked her arm in mine, taking possession of me in a graceful way that evidently pleased Max, for he looked at us smiling.

'Come into the conservatory, Gladys,' whispered Lady Betty in her sister's ear. 'Etta has a cold coming on and will be afraid of following us.'

The conservatory led out of the drawing-room, and was lighted by coloured lamps that gave a pretty effect; it was full of choice flowers, and two or three cane chairs filled up the centre. It was not so warm as the drawing-room certainly, but it was pleasant to sit there in the dim perfumed atmosphere and peep through the open window at the firelight. Miss Darrell followed us to the window with a discontented air.

'I hope you are not going to stay there many minutes, Gladys—you will certainly give yourself and Miss Garston a bad cold if you do. There is something wrong with the warming apparatus, and Giles says it will be some days before it will be properly warmed. I thought I told you so this morning.'

'I do not think Miss Garston will take cold, Etta, and it is very pleasant here;' but though Miss Darrell retreated from the window, I think we all felt as much constrained as though she had joined us, for not a word could escape her ear if she chose to listen.

But this fact did not seem to daunt Lady Betty for long, for she soon began chattering volubly to us both.

'I am not so cross now as I was,' she said frankly. 'I am afraid I was very rude to Mr. Tudor at dinner; but what could I do when Etta was so impertinent? No, she is not there,

Gladys; she has gone out of the room looking as cross as possible. But what do you think she said to me?'

'Never mind telling us what she said, dear,' returned Miss Hamilton, soothingly.

'Oh, but I want to tell Miss Garston—she looks dreadfully curious, and I do not like her to think me cross for nothing. I am not like that, am I, Gladys? Well, just before we went in to dinner, she begged me in a whisper not to talk quite so much to Mr. Tudor as I had done last time. Now, what do you want, Leah?' pulling herself up rather abruptly.

'I have only brought you some shawls, Lady Betty, as Miss Darrell says the conservatory is so cold. She has told Thornton to mention to his master when he takes in the coffee that Miss Gladys is sitting here, and she hopes he will forbid it.'

'You can take away the shawls, Leah,' returned Miss Hamilton, quietly, but there was a scornful look on her pale face as she spoke. 'We are not going to remain here, since Miss Darrell is so anxious about our health. Shall we come in, Miss Garston, perhaps it is a trifle chilly here?' and seeing how the wind blew, and that Miss Darrell was determined to have her way in the matter, I acquiesced silently; but I was not a bit surprised to see Lady Betty stamp her little foot as she followed us.

Miss Darrell was lying back on a velvet lounge, and welcomed us with a provoking smile.

'I thought the threat of telling Giles would bring you in, Gladys,' she said laughing; 'what a foolish child you are to be so reckless of your health. Every one knows Gladys is delicate,' she went on, turning to me, 'everything gives her cold. Giles has been obliged to forbid her attending evening service this winter—you were terribly rebellious about it, were you not, my dear; but, of course, Giles had his way. No one in this house ventures to disobey him.'

Miss Hamilton did not answer, she was standing looking into the fire, and her lips were set firmly as though nothing would make her unclose them.

'Oh, do sit down,' continued her cousin, pettishly; 'it gives one such an uncomfortable feeling when a tall person stands like a statue before one.' And as Miss Hamilton quietly seated herself, she went on, 'Don't you think religious people are far more self-willed than worldly ones, Miss Garston? I daresay you are self-willed yourself. Gladys made as much fuss about giving up evening service as though her salvation depended on her going twice or three times a day. " What is to prevent you reading the service in your own room ? " I used to say to her. " It cannot be your duty to disobey your brother and make yourself ill." '

' The illness lay in your own imagination, Etta,' observed Miss Hamilton, coldly. ' Giles would never have found out my chest was delicate if you had not told him so.'

Miss Darrell gave her favourite little shrug, and inspected her rings.

' See what thanks I get for my cousinly care,' she said good-humouredly. ' I suppose, Gladys, you were vexed with me for telling him that you were working yourself to death —that the close air of the schoolroom made your head ache, and that so much singing was too much for your strength.'

' If you please, Etta, we will talk about some other subject; my health, or want of health, will not interest Miss Garston.' She spoke with dignity, and then, turning to me with a winning smile, 'Giles has told me about your singing. Will you be good enough to sing something to us? It would be a great pleasure; both Lady Betty and I are so fond of music.'

'Miss Garston looks very tired, Gladys; it is almost selfish to ask her,' observed Miss Darrell, softly; and then I knew that Miss Hamilton's request did not please her.

I had vowed to myself that no amount of pressing should induce me to sing that evening, but I could not have refused that gentle solicitation. As I unbuttoned my gloves and took my place at the grand piano, I determined that I would sing anything and everything that Miss Hamilton wished—Miss Darrell should not silence me; and with this resolve hot on me I commenced the opening bars of 'The Lost Chord,' and before I had finished the song Miss Hamilton had crept into the corner beside me, and remained there as motionless as though my singing had turned her into stone.

CHAPTER XVI.

GLADYS.

I DO not know how the majority of people feel when they sing, but with me the love of music was almost a passion. I could forget my audience in a moment, and would be scarcely aware if the room were empty or crowded.

For example, on this evening I had no idea that the gentlemen had entered the room, and the first intimation of the fact was conveyed to me by hearing a 'Bravo!' uttered by Mr. Hamilton under his breath.

'But you must not leave off,' he went on, quite earnestly. 'I want you to treat us as you treat poor Phebe Locke, and sing one song after another until you are tired.'

I was about to refuse this request very

civilly but decidedly, for I had no notion of obeying such an arbitrary command, when Miss Hamilton touched my arm.

'Oh, do please go on singing as Giles says; it is such a pleasure to hear you.' And after this I could no longer refuse.

So I sang one song after another, chiefly from memory, and sometimes I could hear a soft clapping of hands, and sometimes there was breathless silence, and a curious feeling came over me as I sang. I thought that the only person to whom I was singing was Miss Hamilton, and that I was pleading with her to tell me the reason of her sadness, and why there was such a weary, hopeless look in her eyes, when the world was so young with her, and the God-given gift of beauty was hers.

I was singing as though she and I were alone in the room, when Max suddenly whispered in my ear, 'That will do, Ursula,' and as soon as the verse concluded I left off. But before I could rise Miss Darrell was beside us.

'Oh, thank you so much, Miss Garston; you are very amiable to sing so long. Giles was certainly loud in your praises, but I was hardly prepared for such a treat. Why, Gladys, dear, have you been crying? What an impressionable child you are! Miss Garston has not contrived to draw tears from my eyes.'

But without making any reply Miss Hamilton quietly left the room. Were her eyes wet, I wonder? Was that why Max stopped me? Did he want to shield her from her cousin's sharp scrutiny? If so, he failed.

'It is such a pity Gladys is so foolishly sensitive,' she went on, addressing Uncle Max; 'these sort of natures are quite unfit for the stern duties of life. I am quite uneasy about her sometimes, am I not, Giles? Her spirits are so uneven, and she has so little strength. Parochial work nearly killed her, Mr. Cunliffe. You said yourself how ill she looked in the summer.'

'True; but I never thought the work hurt her,' replied Max, rather bluntly. 'I think it was a mistake for Miss Hamilton to give up all her duties; occupation is good for every one.'

'That is my opinion,' observed Mr. Hamilton. 'Etta is always making a fuss about Gladys' health, but I tell her there is not the least reason for alarm; many people not other-

wise delicate take cold easily; it is true I
advised her to give up evening service for a
few weeks until she got stronger.'

'Indeed!' and here Max looked a little
perplexed. 'I thought you told me, Miss
Darrell, that your cousin found our service
too long and wearisome, and this was the
reason she stayed away.'

'Oh, no, you must have misunderstood me,'
returned Miss Darrell, flushing a little. 'Gladys
may have said she liked a shorter sermon in the
evening, but that was hardly her reason for
staying away, at least——'

'Of course not; what nonsense you talk,
Etta,' observed Mr. Hamilton, impatiently.
'You know what a trouble I had to coax
Gladys to stay at home; she was rather ob-
stinate about it—as girls are—but I asked her
as a special favour to myself to remain.'

Max's face cleared up surprisingly, and as
Miss Hamilton at that moment re-entered the
room, he accosted her almost eagerly.

'Miss Hamilton, we have been talking
about you in your absence; your brother and
I have been agreeing that it is really a great
pity that you should have given up all your

parish duties—it is a little hard on us all, is it not, Tudor? Your brother declares occupation will do you good; now I am sure your cousin will not have the slightest objection to give up your old class, and she can take Miss Matthews's, and then I shall have two good workers instead of one.'

For an instant Miss Hamilton hesitated; her face relaxed, and she looked at Max a little wistfully: but Miss Darrell interposed in her sprightly way—

'Do as you like, Gladys dear. Mr. Cunliffe will be too glad of your help, I am sure, as he sees how much you wish it. We all think you are fretting after your old scholars; home duties are not exciting enough, and even Giles notices how dull you are. Oh, you shall have my class with pleasure; anything to see you happy, love; shall we make the exchange to-morrow ?'

'No, thank you, Etta; I think things had better be as they are,' and Miss Hamilton walked away proudly, and spoke to Mr. Tudor; the sudden brightness in her face had dimmed, and I was near enough to see that her hand trembled.

'There you see,' observed Miss Darrell, complacently. 'I have done my best to persuade her in public and private to amuse herself and not give way to her feelings of lassitude—" do a little, but not much," I have often said to her; but with Gladys it must be all or none.'

'Ursula, do you know how late it is?' asked Max, coming up to me. He looked suddenly very tired, and I saw at once that he wished me to go; so I made my adieux as quickly as possible, and in a few minutes we had left the house accompanied by Mr. Tudor.

Uncle Max was very quiet all the way home. I had expected him to be full of questions as to how I had enjoyed my evening, but his only remark was to ask if I were very tired, and then he left me to Mr. Tudor.

'Well, how do you like the folks up at Gladwyn?' demanded Mr. Tudor. 'Lady Betty was not in the best of humours to-night, and hardly deigned to speak to me; but I am sure you must have admired Miss Hamilton.'

'I like both of them,' was my temperate reply; 'you must not be hard on poor little Lady Betty. Miss Darrell had been lecturing her, and that made her cross.'

'So I supposed,' was the prompt answer.
'Well, what did you think of the Dare-all—as
the Vicar calls her sometimes ; is she not like a
pleasant edition of Tupper's " Proverbial Philosophy"—verbose and full of long sentences ?
how many words did she coin to-night, do you
think ?'

There was a little scorn in the young man's
voice. Miss Darrell was evidently not a favourite
in the Vicarage, yet most people would have
called her elegant and well-mannered, and if
she had no beauty, she was not bad-looking.
She was so exceedingly well made up, and her
style of dress was so suitable to her face, that
I was not surprised to hear afterwards from
Lady Betty that many people thought her
cousin Etta handsome. Now when Mr. Tudor
made this spiteful little speech I felt rather
pleased, for my dislike to Miss Darrell had in-
creased rather than diminished by the evening
experiences ; under her smooth speeches there
lurked an antagonistic spirit ; something had
prejudiced her against me even at our first
meeting ; I was convinced that she did not like
me, and would not encourage my visit to
Gladwyn. Mr. Tudor and I talked a good deal

about Lady Betty; he described her as most
whimsical and sound-hearted, half-child and
half-woman, with a touch of the Brownie—her
brother often called her Brownie or little Nix, to
tease her. She was very fond of her sister, he
went on to say, but there was not much companionship between them. Miss Hamilton was
very intellectual, and read a good deal, and
Lady Betty never read anything but novels;
they all made a pet of her—even Mr. Hamilton,
who was not much given to pets—but she was
hardly an influence in the house.

'She has not backbone enough,' he
finished, ' and the Dare-all rules them all with
a rod of iron—" cased in velvet." '

Uncle Max listened to all this in silence,
and as they parted with me at the gate of
the White Cottage he only said ' Good night,
Ursula,' in a depressed voice. He was evidently rather cast down about something;
perhaps Miss Hamilton's decision had disappointed him ; she had been his favourite worker
and had helped him greatly ; he seemed to feel
it hard that she should withdraw her services
so suddenly. How wistfully she had looked at
him as he pleaded with her; it was the first

time I had seen her look at him of her own accord, and yet she had denied his request— very firmly and gently.

'I must be friends with her, and then perhaps she will tell me all about it some day,' I thought—for I was convinced that there was more than met the eye; but it was some time before I could banish these perplexing thoughts.

I saw a good deal of Lady Betty during the next week or two. I met her frequently on my way to the Lockes', and she would walk with me to the gate, and two or three times she made her appearance at the Marshalls'; 'for it's no use calling at the White Cottage of an afternoon,' she would say disconsolately, 'for you are never at home, you inhospitable creature.'

'Why! do you think I live here, Lady Betty?' I returned, smiling. 'Do you know I am becoming a most punctual person. I am always back at the White Cottage by five, and sometimes a little earlier, and I shall always be pleased if you will come in and have tea with me.'

'I should like it of all things,' replied Lady

Betty, with a sigh: ' and I will come sometimes,
you will see if I don't.   But I know Etta will
make a fuss: she always does if I stay out
after dark—and it is dark at four now.   That is
why I pop in here to see you, because Etta is
always busy in the mornings and never takes
any notice of what we do.'

' But surely Miss Darrell will not object
to your coming to see me? ' I asked, somewhat
piqued at this.

' Oh dear no,' returned Lady Betty, jum-
bling her words as though she found my question embarrassing.   ' Etta never objects openly
to anything we do, only she throws stumbling-
blocks in our way.   I do not know why
I have got it into my head that she would not
like Gladys or me to come here without her,
but it is there all the same—the idea, I
mean: it was something she said the other
night to Mrs. Maberley that gave me this
impression.   Mrs. Maberley wanted to call on
you, because she said you were Mr. Cunliffe's
niece, and people ought to take notice of you.
And Etta said, "Oh dear yes; and it was a
very kind thought on Mrs. Maberley's part,
and Mr. Cunliffe would think it so.   That was

why Giles had invited you to Gladwyn; but there was no hurry, and that you evidently were not prepared to enter into society. You had rather strong-minded views on this subject, and that she was not quite sure whether Giles was wise to encourage the intimacy with his sisters." '

'Miss Darrell said this to Mrs. Maberley?'

'Yes. Was it not horrid of Etta? I felt so cross. And Mrs. Maberley is such an old dear: only rather old-fashioned in her notions about girls. So Etta's speech rather frightened her, I could see. Of course she has not called yet? I am almost inclined to tell Giles about it.'

'Indeed, I hope you will do nothing of the kind, Lady Betty. I am sorry Miss Darrell does not like me; but I do not see that it matters so very much what people think of us.'

'Yes; but when Etta takes a dislike to people she tries to prevent us from knowing them, that is the provoking part of it. She is so dreadfully jealous, and I expect it was your singing that gave umbrage. Etta is not at all accomplished; she never cared much for Gladys to sing, because she had such a

sweet voice, and it put her in the background.
Ah! I know how mean it sounds, but it is just
the truth about Etta. And if I were to drop
in for five-o'clock tea, as you say, Leah would
be sure to make her appearance and say I was
wanted at Gladwyn.'

I found Lady Betty's confidential speeches
rather embarrassing, and when I knew her a
little better I took her to task rather seriously
for her want of reticence. But she only
pouted and said, 'When one looks at you,
Miss Garston, one cannot help telling you
things: they all tumble out without one's will.
That is what Gladys means when she says you
have a sympathetic face. I wish you would
get her to talk to you.'

As Lady Betty persisted in haunting the
Marshalls' cottage I determined to make her
useful. So I set her to read to Elspeth, or to
give sewing lessons to Peggy, or to amuse the
younger children, while I was engaged with
my patient; and I soon found that she was a
most helpful little body.

Mr. Hamilton found her sitting in the
kitchen one day surrounded by the children.
She was telling them a story. The baby was

sucking her thumb contentedly on her lap. Poor Mary was worse that day, and I had begged Lady Betty to keep the little ones quiet.

Mr. Hamilton came into the sick-room looking very much pleased. 'I only wish you could make Lady Betty a useful member of society, Miss Garston,' he said, with one of the rare smiles that always lit up his dark face so pleasantly. 'She is a good little thing, but she wants ballast. As a rule, young ladies are terribly idle.'

I had called up at Gladwyn a few days after we had dined there, but to my great disappointment I did not see Miss Hamilton. Miss Darrell was alone, so my visit was as brief as possible.

She told me at once that her cousins had gone over to Brighton for an afternoon's shopping, and that Mr. Hamilton had run up to London for a few hours. And then she commenced plying me with questions in a ladylike way about my work and my past life, but in such a skilful manner that it was almost impossible to avoid answering. She was so sure that I must be dull, living all alone. Oh! of course I was too good and unselfish to say so, but all the same I must be miserably dull. What could have put such a singular idea in my head, she wondered. When young ladies did this sort of thing there was generally some painful reason—they were unhappy at home, or they had had some disastrous love affair. Of course—laughing a little affectedly—she had no intention of hinting at such a reason in my case; any one could see at a glance that I was not that sort of person. I was far too sensible and matter-of-fact: gentlemen would be quite afraid of me, I was so strong-minded. But all the same, she pleaded guilty to a feeling of natural curiosity why such an idea had come into my head.

When I had warded off this successfully—for I declined to enlighten Miss Darrell on this subject—she flew off in a tangent to Aunt Philippa.

'It was such a pity when relations did not entirely harmonise. An aunt could never replace a mother. Ah! she knew that too well; and when there were daughters—and she had heard from Mr. Cunliffe that my cousin Sara was excessively pretty and charming—no doubt there would be natural misunderstandings and jealousies. In spite of all my goodness I was only human. Of course she understood perfectly how it all happened, and she felt very sorry for me.'

I disclaimed the notion of any family disagreement with some warmth, but I do not think she believed me. She had evidently got it into her head that I was a strong-minded young woman with an uncertain temper, who could not live peaceably at home. No doubt she had hinted this to Mrs. Maberley and other ladies. She would make this the excuse for discouraging any degree of intimacy with her cousins. I should not be asked very often to Gladwyn if it depended on Miss Darrell; but Mr. Hamilton had a will of his own, and if he chose me as a companion for his sisters, Miss Darrell would find it difficult to exclude me.

One could see at a glance that Mr. Hamilton was master in his own house. Miss Darrell seemed perfectly submissive to him. There was something almost obsequious in her manner to him. She watched his looks anxiously, and though she coaxed and flattered him, she did not seem quite certain how he would take her speeches.

'We are a strange household; don't you think so, Miss Garston?' she observed presently. 'Giles is our lord and master. None of us poor women dare to contradict him. When dear mamma was alive, she had a great deal of influence over him. He was very fond of her. Her death made a great difference in the house.'

'It must have been a great trouble to you, Miss Darrell.'

'Yes, indeed. I was almost broken-hearted. She had been the dearest and most indulgent of mothers; but Giles was very good to me. Gladys and Lady Betty were very devoted to her; perhaps you have heard them speak of Aunt Margaret. Ah! I forgot, you have only seen Gladys twice,' and here she looked at me rather sharply, but I nodded acquiescence— 'Gladys was always a favourite with her.'

'Miss Hamilton must be a general favourite,' I replied, a little unguardedly.

'Ah! I suppose you think her handsome,' in rather a forced manner; 'many people say she is too pale, and rather too statuesque for their taste.'

'In my opinion she is very beautiful,' I
replied quickly. 'I told Uncle Max the
other day that I thought her face almost
perfect.'

'And what did he say?' she asked rather
eagerly. 'Did he agree with you?' but I was
obliged to confess that I had forgotten his
answer.

'I know Mr. Cunliffe thinks Gladys cold,' she
went on. 'He is too kind-hearted to say so;
but I know he feels hurt at her desertion of her
post. It was a strange whim on her part to give
up all her parish work. I am afraid it was
a little bit of temper. Gladys has a temper,
though you may not think so. She is very firm,
and does not brook the least interference on my
part. Poor dear! if it were not wrong, I
should say she was a little jealous of my influence with Giles, because he likes me to do
things for him; but how am I to help doing
what he asks me, when I owe the very bread
I eat to his kindness?'

Miss Darrell was poor and dependent then.
This piece of news surprised me. I thought of
the glittering rings and silver-mounted dressing-
case and all the luxurious appliances in her

toilet, and wondered if Mr. Hamilton had paid for them.

Miss Darrell seemed to read my thoughts in a most wonderful way.

'Poor mother left very little except personal jewellery. Yes, I owe everything to Giles's generosity. He is good enough to say that I earn my allowance—and indeed I am never idle—but,' interrupting herself, 'I do not want to talk of myself; I am a very insignificant person—just Giles's housekeeper; Gladys is mistress of the house. I only wanted you to explain to Mr. Cunliffe that I am not to blame for Gladys's strange whim. Let me explain a little. She was looking very ill and overworked, and I begged Giles to lecture her. I told him that there was no need for Gladys to do quite so much ; in fact, she was putting herself a little too forward in the parish, considering how young she was, and the Vicar an unmarried man. So Giles and I gave her a word. I am sure he spoke most gently, and I was very careful indeed in only giving her a hint that people, and even Mr. Cunliffe, might misconstrue such devotion. I never saw Gladys in such a passion ; and the next day she had flung everything up. She

told the Vicar that the schoolroom made her
head ache, and that her throat was delicate, and
she could not sing. Poor Mr. Cunliffe was in
such despair, that I was obliged to offer my
services. It is far too much for me, but what
can I do? the parish must not suffer for Gladys's
wilfulness. Now if you could only explain
things a little to Mr. Cunliffe: he looked so hurt
the other night when Gladys refused to take her
old class. No wonder he misses her, for she
used to teach the children splendidly; but if
he knew it was only a little temper on Gladys's
part he would look over it and be friends with
her again. But you must have noticed yourself, Miss Garston, how little he had to say to
her.'

I had found it impossible to check Miss
Darrell's loquacity or to edge in a single word;
but as soon as her breath failed I rose to take
my leave, and she did not seek to detain me.

'You will explain this to Mr. Cunliffe, for
Gladys's sake,' she said, holding my hand. 'I
do want him to think well of her, and I can
see his good opinion is shaken.'

But to this I made no audible reply; but, as
I shook off the dust of Gladwyn, I told myself

y 2

that Uncle Max should not hear Miss Darrell's version from my lips. She wished to make me a tool in her hands; but her breach of confidence had a very different result to what she expected. Miss Darrell's words had cleared up a perplexity in my mind; I could read between the lines, and I fully exonerated Miss Hamilton.

The following afternoon I had a most unexpected pleasure. When I came back to the cottage after my day's work Mrs. Barton met me at the door and told me that Miss Hamilton was in the parlour.

I had thought she meant Lady Betty; but to my surprise I found Miss Hamilton seated by the fire. A pleased smile came to her face as I greeted her most warmly. She must have seen how glad I was; but she shrank back rather nervously when I begged her to take off her furred mantle and stay to tea.

She was not sure that she could remain. Lady Betty was alone, as Giles and Etta were dining at the Maberleys'. She had been asked, and had refused; but Etta had taken in her work, as Mrs. Maberley had wanted them to go early. Perhaps she had better not stay, as it would not be kind to Lady Betty. But I soon overruled this objection. I told Miss Hamilton that I saw Lady Betty frequently, but that she herself had never called since her first visit, and that now I could not let her go.

I think she wanted me to press her; she was arguing against her own wishes, it was easy to see that. By-and-by she asked me in a low voice if I were sure to be alone, or if I expected any visitors; and when I had assured her decidedly that no one but Uncle Max ever came to see me, and that I knew he was engaged this evening, her last scruple seemed to vanish, and she settled herself quite comfortably for a chat. We talked for a little while on indifferent subjects. She told me about the neighbourhood and the people who lived in the large houses by the church, and about her brother's work in the parish, and how if rich people sent for him he always kept them waiting while he went to the poor ones.

'Giles calls himself the poor people's doctor—he attends them for nothing. He cannot always refuse rich people if they will have him, but he generally sends them to Dr. Ramsbotham. You see he never takes money for his services, and as people know this they are ashamed to send for him; and yet they want him because he is so clever. Giles is so fond of his profession; he is always regretting that he had a fortune left him, for he says it would have been far pleasanter to have made one. Giles never did care for money; he is ready to fling it away to any one who asks him.'

Miss Hamilton kept up this desultory talk all teatime. She spoke with great animation about her brother, and I could hardly believe it was the same girl who had sat so silently at the head of the table that evening at Gladwyn. The sad abstracted look had left her face. It seemed as though for a little while she was determined to forget her troubles.

When Mrs. Barton had taken away the tea-tray, she asked me, with the same wistful look in her eyes, to sing to her if I were not tired, and I complied at once.

I sang for nearly half an hour, and then I returned to the fireside. I saw that Miss Hamilton put up her hand to shield her face from the light; but I took no notice, and after a little while she began to talk.

'I never heard any singing like yours, Miss Garston; it is a great gift. There is something different in your voice to any one else's; it seems to touch one's heart.'

'If my singing always makes you sad, Miss Hamilton, it is a very dubious gift.'

'Ah! but it is a pleasant sadness,' she replied quickly. 'I feel as though some kind friend were sympathising with me when you sing; it tells me too that, like myself, you have known trouble.'

I sighed as I looked at Charlie's picture. Her eyes followed my glance, and I saw again that tremulous motion of her hands.

'Yes, I know,' she said hurriedly; but her beautiful eyes were full of tears. 'I have always been so sorry for you. You must feel so lonely without him.'

The intense sympathy with which she said these few words seemed to break down my reserve. In a moment I had forgotten that we were strangers, as I told her about my love for Charlie, and the dear old life at the Rectory.

It was impossible to doubt the interest with which she listened to me. If I paused for an instant, she begged me very gently to tell her more about myself. She was so sorry for me; but it did her good to hear me.

When I spoke of the life at Hyde Park
Gate, and told her how little I was fitted for
that sort of existence, she put down her
shielding hand, and looked at me with strange
wistfulness.

'No, you are too real, too much in earnest,
to be satisfied with that sort of life. Mr.
Cunliffe used to tell us so. And I seemed to
understand it all before I saw you. I always
felt as though I knew you, even before we
met. I hope,' hesitating a little, 'that we
shall see a great deal of you. I know Giles
wishes it.'

'You cannot come here too often, Miss
Hamilton. It will always be such a pleasure
to me to see you.'

'Oh! I did not mean that,' she returned
nervously. 'I may not be able to come here,
—that is, not alone ; there are reasons, and you
must not expect me ; but I hope you will come
to Gladwyn whenever you have an hour to
spare. Giles said so the other day. I think
he meant you to be friends with us. You must
not mind,' getting still more nervous, 'if Etta
is a little odd sometimes. Her moods vary,
and she does not always make people feel as

though they were welcome; but it is only manner, so you must not mind it.'

'Oh no; I shall hope to come and see you and Lady Betty some time.'

'And,' she went on hurriedly, 'if there is anything that I can do to help you, I hope you will tell me so. Perhaps I cannot visit the people; but there are other things—needle-work, or a little money. Oh! I have so much spare time, and it will be such a pleasure.'

'Oh yes; you shall help me,' I returned cheerfully, for she was looking so extremely nervous that I wanted to reassure her; but we were prevented from saying any more on this subject, for just then we heard the click of the little gate, and the next moment Uncle Max walked into the room.

END OF THE FIRST VOLUME.

S.

Spottiswoode & Co. Printers, New-street Square, London.

Bentley's Favourite Novels.

Each work can be had separately, price 6s., of all Booksellers in Town or Country.

By Mrs. HENRY WOOD.

East Lynne. (140th Thousand.)
Anne Hereford.
Bessy Rane.
The Channings.
Court Netherleigh.
Dene Hollow.
Edina.
Elster's Folly.
George Canterbury's Will.
Johnny Ludlow (1st Series).
Johnny Ludlow (2nd Series).
Lady Adelaide.
Life's Secret, A.
Lord Oakburn's Daughters.
Master of Greylands.
Mildred Arkell.
Mrs. Halliburton's Troubles.
Orville College.
Oswald Cray.
Parkwater.
Pomeroy Abbey.
Red Court Farm.
Roland Yorke.
    (A Sequel to 'The Channings.')
Shadow of Ashlydyat.
St. Martin's Eve.
    (A Sequel to 'Mildred Arkell.')
Trevlyn Hold.
Verner's Pride.
Within the Maze.

By FRANCES M. PEARD.

Near Neighbours.

By RHODA BROUGHTON.

Belinda.
Cometh up as a Flower.
Good-bye, Sweetheart!
Joan. | Nancy.
Not Wisely but too Well.
Red as a Rose is She.
Second Thoughts.

By Mrs. ALEXANDER.

Look before you Leap.
Her Dearest Foe.
The Admiral's Ward.
The Executor.
The Freres.
The Wooing o't.
Which shall it be?

By Mrs. ANNIE EDWARDES.

A Ball Room Repentance.
Leah: a Woman of Fashion.
Ought We to Visit Her?
A Girton Girl.

By W. E. NORRIS.

Thirlby Hall.

By Mrs. RIDDELL.

Berna Boyle.
George Geith of Fen Court.
Susan Drummond.

By Mrs. PARR.

Adam and Eve.
Dorothy Fox.

By HAWLEY SMART.

Breezie Langton.

ANONYMOUS.

The Last of the Cavaliers.

London: RICHARD BENTLEY & SON, New Burlington Street,
Publishers in Ordinary to Her Majesty the Queen.

www.ingramcontent.com/pod-product-compliance
Lightning Source LLC
Chambersburg PA
CBHW031338070726
47496CB00017B/1273